Peter Cunningham is from Waterford, Ireland's oldest city. He is the author of the Monument series, widely acclaimed novels set in a fictional version of his home town. His novel, *The Taoiseach* was a controversial best seller; *The Sea and the Silence* won the prestigious Prix de l'Europe. He is a member of Aosdána, the Irish academy of arts and letters, and lives with his wife, not far from Dublin.

Also by Peter Cunningham

The Monument Series
Tapes of the River Delta
Consequences of the Heart
Love in one Edition
The Sea and the Silence

Novels
The Taoiseach
Capital Sins
Who Trespass Against Us
Sister Caravaggio (as editor and contributor)
The Trout

Acts of Allegiance

Peter Cunningham

SANDSTONEPRESS
HIGHLAND | SCOTLAND

First published in Great Britain and Ireland in 2017
This edition 2018

Sandstone Press Ltd
Dochcarty Road
Dingwall
Ross-shire
IV15 9UG
Scotland

www.sandstonepress.com

"Alone Again (Naturally)" written by Gilbert O'Sullivan.
Published by SonyATV Music Publishing / Grand Upright Music Ltd.
Lyrics reproduced with the kind permission of Gilbert O'Sullivan

The publisher acknowledges subsidy from
Creative Scotland towards publication of this volume.

ISBN: 978-1-912240-30-2
ISBNe: 978-1-910985-51-9

Cover design by Mark Swan
Typeset by Iolaire Typography Ltd, Newtonmore
Printed and bound by Totem, Poland

In memory

*PFC
and
RCAC and MFC*

Looking back over the years
And whatever else that appears
I remember I cried when my father died
Never wishing to hide the tears
And at sixty-five years old
My mother, God rest her soul
Couldn't understand why the only man
She had ever loved had been taken
Leaving her to start with
A heart so badly broken
Despite encouragement from me
No words were ever spoken
And when she passed away
I cried and cried all day
Alone again, naturally

Gilbert O'Sullivan

Prologue

The Recent Past

He calls it the explosion. Not the bomb, or the outrage. The explosion. He always describes it in the same way: an ear-sucking frenzy that bursts from shops and houses and lacerates the air. A towering force in which bicycles and books are bizarrely suspended. He recounts how he is rammed face down to the road, how the earth tilts sharply, like the deck of a listing ship, so that he feels he is slipping off, and grabs at the egg-smeared cobbles to save himself. He describes how his ears whine at high pitch, and how, when he regains his feet, choking, he can hear distant geese in fright, and only gradually realises they are house alarms. His account of how he stumbles through the slabs of dust – blood in his mouth, never wanting to arrive, reciting old prayers, begging for mercy – is always the same.

She listens respectfully, as if hearing it all for the first time; then, gently, they resume.

They follow a routine. After breakfast, they sit, she at her writing table, he in his armchair overlooking the garden. He speaks and she transcribes in her commendably neat hand; following which, they eat the lunch she has prepared, and then he naps. Afterwards, in the afternoon, she reads to him what she transcribed earlier. Later, they go out on to the deck at the back, beside the unused swimming pool, and sit together with a drink.

Some mornings, they are interrupted in their tasks, for example, when the intercom sounds – a loud peremptory buzzing, the signal from the security people up on the road that a food delivery has arrived; or that the pool-cleaning contractor is on his way down; or that the taxi bearing Maria Fernanda, who cleans on Saturday mornings, will shortly appear. Three sets of locks secure the door, and they have to be opened one by one. But only after the intercom has sounded. That is the procedure.

Part I

Part I

1

Summer 1964

The sound of tennis being played in the Irish countryside in July was infinitely reassuring. I lay in the hammock, a newspaper on my face, hearing the pock-pock-pock, and the voices that followed the conclusion of a point, and their light laughter. Then, if I pointed my senses, like a sniper, I could fasten upon bees in the fuchsias, a tractor turning hay a mile away, and the fussy murmur of the stream as it oozed downhill beyond the tennis court and into the lake.

'I do believe that was out, Sugar!'

'I saw chalk, Christopher.'

'I saw no chalk – but very well. Your point.'

Christopher had been trying to beat Sugar for years, and had carried her racquets when she had played as a junior at Wimbledon. His father, a medical man, had relocated from Ireland to a practice in Devon before the war; now Christopher worked for a bank in London, where, it seemed, promotion eluded him.

5

Tinkling cups meant that Alison was approaching. Large, jolly and pretty, Alison was as dynamic as Christopher was not. She had brought an inheritance to their marriage, a fact that Christopher, when drunk, sometimes guffawed about.

'Two sets to love down and still he won't give in,' she said.

I sat up. 'I've given up trying to beat her.'

'Christopher's been trying since he was six.'

'I know.'

'I'm not waiting for them,' she said and began to pour.

Christopher and Alison were staying with us, as they had previously, on their way to their holiday home in County Kerry. Sometimes, when my mind was elsewhere, I looked up and found Alison inspecting me, but her instant smile forgave everything, and those moments, whatever they were, always passed.

'How's the job?' She picked up her cup and saucer and sat on the hammock beside me.

'A lot of pen-pushing.'

'But you like it.'

'Who could possibly like a job that involves negotiating tariffs?'

'Mindless, I know.'

'I do it for the money.'

'As do we all.'

'All I think about is how I can manage to get back here permanently.'

'Who wouldn't adore this?' she said.

Her MP father had once chaired a Commons committee inquiring into ground rents, and Alison's first job had been as his researcher, she had told me when we'd first met, three years before. I could understand how, having arrived that summer in Ireland for the first time, Alison would have seen us no differently to other families she would have known, in Berkshire or Somerset, the lovely setting of house and lands little different to those in England, the economy casting shadows over conversations. Ireland seemed nothing like a foreign country to her; yet the fact that it was clearly intrigued her.

'We don't really know much about you lot, do we?' was a remark I remembered. It was a general comment, embracing the English on the one hand, and the Irish on the other, but it could also have meant something more specific.

'You should talk to Christopher.'

'Oh, God, he knows nothing.'

It was true, for Christopher was hopeless when it came to Ireland, having been brought up in a world of attitudes where one pretended to know little about Irish politics, and in Christopher's case the pretence was unnecessary. From then on, in summer, when the Chases and their two girls came to stay, our conversations were designed by Alison to provide her with insights into Ireland. That we each worked for a government made us one of a kind, even if the most I learned of her job was that she was employed in some capacity by the Home Office.

Thick wedges of insects hovered above the lake, each wedge a tumultuous universe. From the summerhouse, Nurse Fleming, our nanny, emerged, pushing our little son in his pram, with Alison's two girls skipping alongside.

'Christopher loves it here,' Alison said. 'I think he regrets his father ever left.'

'We all want to go back to our childhood, or so they say.'

'Sometimes when he's had too much to drink, he says that, if he'd stayed, he would have married Sugar.'

7

'Then what would you and I have done?' I heard myself ask.

As the hammock swung gently, its motion governed by my heels, and Alison stuck out her legs and kicked off her shoes, I felt my ears occluding the way they always did in the presence of danger.

'An interesting thought,' she said, leaning back, and allowing me to feel her warm thigh. From the partly hidden lake, by a miracle of acoustics, came the sound of wine being poured into a glass.

'They've gone out in the punt,' she said drowsily.

I didn't respond, but neither did I draw away, which was in itself my reply to the simple message she wished to convey, our little secret suddenly hatched. But much more than just physical attraction was at work, for I knew then, and with a transfixing jolt, that Alison understood me.

'Oh, by the way,' she said, as if she had just remembered, 'I met a chap the other day who says he knows you.'

I could barely hear her as my head spun. 'Really?'

'Vance – can't remember his first name. Reddish hair, amusing. Said you were at school together.'

'Vance,' I said and drank my tea.

'We were discussing summer holidays, and when I mentioned Ireland, he said, "I was at school with someone from Ireland who lives in mountains near the south-east coast." Had to be you.'

'What does … Vance … do with himself?'

'Foreign Office, I believe.'

From the water came the edge-clear voices of Christopher and Sugar, and the splash of oars as he rowed and she cast. I sat in the ebbing light, more miserable than I had ever been.

8

'Are you happy, Marty?'

I could not bring myself to look at her. 'You mean...?'

'I'm not trying to seduce you. I mean, generally, is it all making sense for you? Are you fulfilled in your work? Are you in the place you really want to be?'

The tide of my heart lapped. 'I sometimes feel...'

'Go on.'

I suddenly wanted to talk about my father, which I knew was pathetic; to explain the standards and values I had been brought up to believe in; to describe the great unsatisfied yearning in my heart and the emptiness in which I partly lived. I knew, I just knew, she would understand it if I told her that, despite having a good job and being married to a beautiful woman, there were aspects of my life in which I was abjectly lonely. But how could I tell a near stranger that I needed something I could hardly begin to explain?

'Oh, it's just nonsense,' I said. 'It's nothing.'

'I think I understand,' she said quietly, 'and I think I can help you.'

I laughed, a little too loudly.

'Help you do the right thing,' she said. 'The right thing for you. I can give your life the meaning I think it needs.'

My terror and exhilaration surged so strongly, side by side, that I felt dizzy.

'There's really nothing to worry about, you know,' Alison said. 'Trust me. No one will ever know.'

Nurse Fleming was bringing the child over to say goodnight.

'I...think we should join the others,' I said.

As we got up, a coot scampered across a wad of lily pads and left them heaving in its wake.

2

Foothills On The Way To Waterford

Even as a child, I could savour the constituent parts of each furlong of the journey to Waterford. It began with the departure from Waterloo's inner yard, the undertone of bantam hens in the hayloft, the crunch of tyres on gravel, all too brief, for I was ever seized at that moment by the sweet sorrow of departure, by the dread of leaving all I knew and loved.

The drive that lay ahead – an itinerary laid down from my infancy – squeezed me gently from the house and its surroundings. A little bridge crossed the lake neck, and, without warning, as it were, for each time it seemed a surprise, we were climbing steeply, and as I looked back I could see the lake far below, pellucid in summer light, dazzling and unique.

As soon as sight of Waterloo was lost, we began to cross the long, sandy ridge, car windows down, broom scent around us, the antics of rabbits as sideshows. Often, it rained without warning, a completely local event; in fact, on those days we did not encounter a shower on the way to Waterford we took it as a bad omen, for showers in the foothills always foretold sunshine in the town below. At this point, I could never resist lighting a cigarette, a ritual within a ritual, something my father had always done, and the scent of tobacco in that setting brought the old man back for an instant, like a genie.

At the ridge end, now quietly rising, the twinkling river mouth brimmed into view. As a child, I had thought of this as a moving picture, which was intensely exciting, for with each new revolution the vista grew below us, and the bright green of the mountain drained into a darker, deeper colour, almost blue, as it swooped down to meet the cluster of the town and the river. We always pulled in then, since the high walls of the rock fissure in which we now paused – which we called the 'Door', because it seemed to divide one world from another – was thick with gorse, which in summer drenched our senses as we perched, reluctant to leave but at the same time excited by what lay ahead.

We began to roll down through the ever-changing shades and glinting light made by mountain rivulets flowing through heather. If my father was at the wheel, he always cut the car's engine at this point, to save petrol, and we freewheeled, making each time a test of skill to see how far the car could be urged forward without the engine, the railway station being generally accepted as the limit of possibility.

3

November 1951

From the gardens behind the houses in Fowler Street, an aspect could be enjoyed over steeples and huddled roofs to the uplifting expanse of the River Suir, and beyond it into County Kilkenny.

'Optimism is hard to find nowadays,' said Bobby Gillece.

Although he had removed his topcoat, Bobby preferred to stand, one boot in the hall, leaning on the door jamb to the sitting room. Everyone, me included, knew what was really on Bobby's mind, because he kept glancing to the street door, his flourishing ginger moustache twitching like a cat's whiskers.

'No money around for anything,' he said.

'Run for the Corporation and you'll skate in,' said the Gent with several nods of his shining head. 'Skate in.'

Dying light filtered through the net curtain turning Granny Kane into a watchful corpse.

'The whole ward will vote for you,' the Gent scowled, defying anyone to disagree.

12

The week before, my parents had taken the steamer from Waterford to Fishguard, en route to London, for what my father had described as an urgent business trip. Waterloo had been boarded and locked, the staff had been sent home and I had been taken out of school and sent to stay with Granny Kane.

'The war put us on our knees, and we weren't even in it,' said Bobby Gillece, shifting to make way for Auntie Angela as she carried through a laden tea tray. 'Although maybe now we should have been.'

When Bobby spoke, his decaying upper teeth were visible, despite his moustache.

'That's a good one coming from you,' the Gent said.

'You move with the times, you move with the times,' Bobby said.

'Ho-ho!'

Uncle Ted, freshly washed, in a clean white shirt, appeared from the kitchen.

'Bobby was just saying we'd have been better off if we'd been in the war,' said the Gent and rolled his eyes. He operated a small abattoir at the bottom of the hill, where the wails of dying pigs could be heard three days a week.

'All I said was, you move with the times,' Bobby said.

'A lot of money moving north of the border since the war,' Uncle Ted said and settled into the armchair just inside the door. 'A lot of money.'

'And you would know what's happening north of the border,' said the Gent with mild sarcasm.

'American money,' Uncle Ted said, 'American money. I'm listening to them talking about it up there every night.'

'Put the doily under the pot, Angela,' said Granny Kane.

Granny's terraced house was one room wide and two rooms deep, with a kitchen tacked on behind. The narrow hall, in which Bobby partly was standing, was floored with tiles; the staircase to the floors above was covered in a carpet that my aunts had laboured on for years, snagging little loops of red wool on to a cloth backing.

'Pa bought pigs up there in the old days,' said the Gent and became temporarily unfocused, his right knee bobbing with a life of its own. 'Before any border.'

'God give him peace,' Granny Kane said.

'Up there a lot of them still think there's no border,' said Uncle Ted with a quick smile and Bobby Gillece laughed.

Wide-shouldered and tall, Uncle Ted owned a coal round that supplied that part of Waterford. When I first saw him hoisting a heavy bag of coal on each shoulder, I just knew he was the strongest man I had ever seen.

Auntie Angela laid the cups, saucers, spoons, linen napkins, the teapot and a silver tea-strainer on the table, and went back out to the kitchen with her head down. Amplified radio static could suddenly be heard upstairs, like a series of small explosions.

'Turn it down, Iggy!' Uncle Ted shouted.

'Jesus! If that young fellow blows the fuses again, I'll brain him,' said the Gent.

'Boys will be boys,' Granny Kane said. 'Isn't that right, Marty?'

I began to blush. I was shy and hated it when people noticed me.

'Where are Marty's mammy and daddy?' asked Bobby Gillece, all innocence.

'In England. On business,' said the Gent, closely examining his fingernails.

'Where do they go to in England, son?' Bobby asked and I could see the slyness in his look.

'To London,' I replied.

'London,' said Bobby gravely. 'Hmmm. A big city.'

'Pa went to White City once,' Granny said. 'To back a dog.'

'My father has business interests in London,' I said.

'And what business interests might those be?' asked Bobby and winked in the Gent's direction.

'I'm sure he'll tell you himself the next time you meet him,' said Granny with a thrust of her little chin.

'Only enquiring, only enquiring,' said Bobby.

'Marty likes it here; he goes to school with Iggy,' said Uncle Ted. 'Two cousins sharing the same desk. Isn't that right, Marty?'

'Yes, Uncle Ted.'

'He's got some build on him for a young fellow,' said Bobby Gillece, and his gaze, curious and lingering, hung on me for an uncomfortable moment. 'How old is he at all?'

'I'll be eleven at Christmas,' I said, the way I knew my father would have.

'Eleven,' said Bobby in wonder, as if my age had now joined a list of matters that needed to be explained. 'Some size for eleven.'

Auntie Angela reappeared with the next instalment of the afternoon tea, just as Iggy ducked beneath her tray. Auntie Angela let out a tiny scream.

'You little fairy!' said Ted and playfully batted Iggy's ears.

My first cousin was small for his age, with straight fair hair, a noticeably square head and high cheekbones that stood out beneath restless blue eyes. He held out his hand to Granny.

'Ah, will you look, another one,' said Granny without enthusiasm and briefly inspected the tiny wooden cat that Iggy had made upstairs. 'Thank you, Ignatius.'

'He's a very good boy,' said his father, pulling Iggy to him. He caught his son's face in his big hands and kissed him. 'How are the babies at all?'

'She's feeding them,' Iggy said, then turned and looked intently at me.

'I don't like them in the house,' sniffed Granny, her little mouth crimped into a tight purse. 'I hate the smell of them.'

Iggy's penetrating stare switched between me and Granny Kane. His mother, one of Uncle Ted's customers, had fled to London after his birth, preferring the dangers of the Blitz to the scorn Waterford held for an unwed mother, I had heard it remarked.

'Give out the napkins first, Angela,' said Granny.

The front door could be heard opening in a squelch of draught-proofing, and Bobby Gillece's head snapped to the right.

'Ho-ho!' said Uncle Ted.

'Is that Stanley?' Granny asked.

'Hel-*lo*!' Auntie Kate was rubbing her hands. 'It's *cold* out there.'

'Come into the fire, Kate,' said Granny. 'Where's Stanley?'

'How would I know, Mother?'

'He said he'd be back in ten minutes an hour ago.'

'He'll be grand, Mam,' Uncle Ted said with his quick, disarming smile.

'He brought me in a bucket of coal an hour ago and I haven't seen him since,' Granny said.

'Hello, Bobby,' said Auntie Kate as if she'd just noticed him. 'You mustn't be very busy today.'

'I am busy,' Bobby Gillece said. 'Very busy. I just called in to say hello.'

'Start without me,' Auntie Kate said as she went to the kitchen and I was presented with a brief glimpse of her nice legs.

'We'll come out of this one day,' said the Gent, taking a cup of tea from Auntie Angela. 'In the meantime, go for the Corporation. You'll skate in.'

Bobby Gillece's longing gaze was fixed towards the kitchen.

'No thanks,' he said when Auntie Angela tried to hand him a cup and saucer, 'I have to get back to work.'

'Have a cup of tea, Bobby,' said Granny.

'No, thanks, honestly, Mrs Kane. I have to get back,' said Bobby, although he did not seem to want to. 'We have a contents auction on Monday.'

Iggy and I, sitting on the floor beside Uncle Ted, shared a plate of cake and were served our tea in china mugs. Iggy looked over at me and smiled. Upstairs in the bedroom, where he slept with his father, was a workbench with assorted radio transceivers and a soldering iron. Above the bench was pinned a photograph of three youths, in their teens, their caps pulled low, standing beside the running boards of a Morris Oxford Saloon. Each of them had a pistol stuck into his belt. Someone had scrawled 'The Flying Squad – 1939' on the bottom of the photograph. Iggy had told me that the youth on the left was his dad. On the other side of the car, in those days without a moustache, stood Bobby Gillece, who was Iggy's godfather. The face of the third gunman was slightly blurred and Iggy did not know his name.

'Marty might give me and Iggy a hand some days after school,' Uncle Ted said, 'coming up to Christmas.'

'Oh, I'm not sure if that...' Granny Kane began.

Auntie Kate came in and crouched beside us, her bare knees level with my chin. She had recently started work in the Munster & Leinster Bank. 'So, how are my two boyfriends?' she asked and ran her fingers through my hair and Iggy's. Over her shoulder I could see Bobby Gillece's Adam's apple rise and fall. 'What have you two been up to?'

'My cat had eight kittens,' Iggy said, and suddenly smiled, 'but only three lived.'

'Ah, dear,' said Auntie Kate. 'But sure, that's the way it goes, isn't it?'

'Best kitten is a drowned kitten,' said Granny.

'I'm not drowning them,' Iggy said.

'Don't speak like that to Granny,' said Uncle Ted.

Although Iggy was staring at the floor, I could see his eyes going at speed, back and forth.

Bobby Gillece straightened himself. 'I must be off.'

'If you see Stanley, tell him to come home,' said Granny, which seemed to make up Bobby's mind for him.

'I will, Mrs Kane, of course I will,' he said and prepared to leave.

'I worry about his chest when he's out this long,' Granny said.

'He's a grown man, Mother,' said the Gent.

'He's got a weak chest,' Granny said. 'He picks up anything that's going.'

'I'll keep an eye out for him, Mrs Kane,' said Bobby. 'I'll bring him back here myself if I see him.'

'Wrap up, Bobby,' Auntie Kate said as she poured tea and sat on the arm of her mother's chair.

Bobby's face flooded with gratitude and his teeth came into view. 'I might drop in later,' he said.

'Tell your mother I was asking for her,' said Granny.

'Bobby's a racing certainty if he runs for the Corporation,' said the Gent as the front door closing confirmed Bobby's departure. 'I don't know what's stopping him.'

'He never stops talking, that's for sure,' said Uncle Ted.

'He's very good to Stanley,' said the Gent. 'Buys him sweets, doesn't let corner boys bully him.'

'I just wish Stanley was home,' Granny said.

'Right.' Auntie Kate put down her cup and saucer. 'Marty and Iggy, put on your coats, go out and find Uncle Stanley and tell him he is to come home immediately.'

4

WATERFORD

November 1951

The tang of salt and bottom mud rode the east-blown river air. By the wall in Jail Street, a chew-eared tabby cat oozed away.

'Here, puss, puss!' Iggy called.

In the Christian Brothers, where I sat beside him, Iggy was beaten on the hands with a thick leather strap. These almost daily punishments arose from him failing to read aloud properly, or at all, in either English or Irish, or failing, or refusing, to write in those languages. Iggy's seeming indifference to being flogged drove our celibate teacher to new heights of venom. My cousin's expression of watchful awareness changed little during these beatings, although when the brother hoisted him off the floor by the hair, Iggy did cry out.

We ambled into the yard on Jail Street, with its lean-to, where Uncle Ted kept coal for bagging and his piebald mare. The smell of horse dung was strangely comforting and reminded me of the yard in Waterloo. Inside the shed, a square chimney breast soared to a shelf on which a blacksmith's rusting anvil had been placed, presumably to make room for coal. Iggy scampered up the black escarpment and edged out along the shelf. From behind the anvil he lifted a jam jar half-full of toffees.

'I steal them from Uncle Stanley,' he said as we sat, legs dangling. Through a gap in the slates, I could make out the spire of the Dominicans.

'What if he comes in here and finds them?' I asked.

Iggy gave me one of his looks. 'He can't climb, stupid. When he follows me, I come up here and eat his sweets so he can see me. When he starts to shout, I throw coal at him.'

I could not understand why Iggy would not want to learn to read and write, but the fact that he did not, and was prepared to suffer for it, made him a hero to me. And if I said, 'Why don't you read it when the brother asks you?' Iggy would look at me pityingly, as he had just done.

'Maybe he's fallen into the river and drowned,' Iggy said and unwrapped a toffee. 'Or maybe he's swallowed his tongue. My da says Uncle Stanley sometimes swallows his tongue. My da says we might soon be moving to south Armagh.'

'My father says we may move to London,' I said, recalling late-night discussions in Waterloo. 'He does business there.'

Iggy scoffed. 'In Armagh we'll have our own house and a farm with chickens and pigs,' he said, as if the life that awaited him would always be better than anything I could come up with.

It would be years before I learned that Iggy Kane, who had nearly died from measles as an infant, was severely dyslexic, an affliction unrecognised in 1950s' Ireland. Uncle Ted ignored the complaints from the school: he had seen his son at the workbench upstairs, making tiny cat sculptures from lumps of wood, or helping him to rebuild the RAF Bomber Command receiver that Uncle Ted had bought from someone in Omagh.

'D'you know Granny Kane has to wipe Uncle Stanley's arse?'

'What?' I cried.

Iggy laughed. 'I seen her. Auntie Kate is nice, though, isn't she?'

The mention of Auntie Kate raised in me sudden new yearnings.

'Bobby Gillece likes her, I think.'

'Of course he likes her, stupid,' Iggy said, and climbed to his feet. 'She gives me money and I let her hug me.'

I caught the anvil to pull myself up and it teetered alarmingly.

'Bobby Gillece gives me money too,' Iggy remarked as we clambered down the hill of coal and the mare let out a blast of alarm, 'but I don't let him hug me, although he wants to.'

'I'd hate it if he hugged me,' I said.

'He kissed me once, in the kitchen, and then gave me sixpence,' Iggy said. 'His breath smells like shit.'

I was never given money, I reflected; in fact, accepting money from anyone was strictly forbidden at home and, on one occasion, when a visitor to Waterloo had given me a half-crown as thanks for my giving up my bed, and I had proudly shown what I had been given when he was gone, the Captain had grabbed the coin, rushed outside like a crazy man, and thrown it in the lake.

Although I was much bigger and broader than him, and could hold my own easily in playground fights, I longed for Iggy's acceptance. Unlike me, he lived in a world free of instructions, except at school, and there he ignored them. Where other boys used their fists to protect themselves, or their voices to protest, all Iggy's armour lay in his penetrating light blue eyes. Those eyes, which saw only jumbles of incoherent symbols on a page, and which could make no sense of the shapes he was required to make with a pen, comprehended instantly how to strip a transformer out of an old radio and use the insulated copper wiring as a receiving antenna.

5

WATERLOO FARM

1951

Our home had begun as a stone cottage, but over the course of a century a number of additions had been made, in some cases on two levels. Outside, a stable yard and sheds had gone up, one by one. The result was a straggling collection of buildings tacked on to the side of a mountain. The farm had been purchased by my mother's great-grandfather, Hubert Ransom from Dover, a government land surveyor, who had mapped the land around our mountain for the first time on the day of the Battle of Waterloo. He decided there and then to become a farmer, and bought the holding for the price of a first-class railway ticket from London to Liverpool, the story went.

My grandfather Ransom had commanded respect in the area, despite his eccentricities, which included making his own clothes and always walking into Waterford, despite the fact that he could have ridden. Nancy, my mother, was the last of that line; Paddy, my father, was Paddy Kane from Fowler Street, Waterford, but in deference to the looming extinction of the Ransom name in those parts, when he married he changed his name to Ransom. Soon afterwards, when I was born, he joined the British Army, took part in the liberation of Europe and reached the rank of Captain. My mother told me in later years that the war had changed my father, turned him inside out. It was to his great credit that he had survived it, she said, but in order to do so, he had had to change. He returned to Waterloo as Captain Ransom, and became known as the Captain, an entirely different person to Paddy Kane who had left Waterford a few years earlier.

Apparently the Captain had wanted to have me baptised in the Church of Ireland, like the Ransoms, but my grandfather, Pa Kane, had got wind of the plan. A delegation sent out from Waterford told my father that he had a week to bring me into the Catholic cathedral or Waterloo would be burned to the ground.

It was all gloriously disorganised. Bantam hens thronged the haylofts, lambs and pigs wandered the yard and in summer store cattle were left, more or less, to their own devices. Two staff were employed: Danny, who groomed the horses and fed cattle in winter, and Eileen, from Glenmore, who cooked, cleaned, washed and ironed. Danny lived nearby and was paid erratically; Eileen, who lived with us, came from very poor circumstances, and was seldom paid, on the basis that she was being housed and fed, and that her position was more of a privilege than a job. She had pushed me in my pram, and fed and changed me, and had been the one who saw me take my first steps. As I grew older, she hovered around the fringes of my presence with an anxiety that greatly annoyed the Captain.

'Christ, that bloody woman drives me mad!'

Danny occasionally took off after tea and returned in the dark with a horny mountain ewe, whose throat he'd slit and, having saved its blood in buckets, hung from a beam, and skinned. The sheep's vividly naked body steamed gently. Later, Danny laid it out in the kitchen where Eileen butchered it. Danny then packed the meat in a barrel of salt.

Danny encouraged me to steal my parents' cigarettes, which we smoked together in the orchard, or behind the wall of the pigsty. My dog, Oscar, a collie mongrel that Danny had found in Mullinavat, curled at my feet as I learned to inhale. Danny was easily moved to discuss women at such moments, all of whom he described, even those he admired, as cunts.

It was sometimes hard for me to grasp that the Captain's mother was Granny Kane and that the people who lived in Fowler Street were his brothers and sisters. Although once or twice in Waterford, when I had been with him, he had met Uncle Ted for a drink and told me later that Ted was his favourite brother, in general he preferred not to talk about his family, even when I came home from Fowler Street with enough sausages and bacon to keep Waterloo fed for a month. I once remarked that I liked his sister, Auntie Kate.

'Hmm,' he said.

'Granny says she is going to marry Bobby Gillece.'

'Mister Gillece,' my father corrected.

'Mister Gillece.'

'Not my kind of chap,' the Captain said.

I knew better than to ask why. It was more productive

to discuss matters such as the war, or Winston Churchill, or London.

'Dad, how does a sniper work?'

He narrowed his gaze. 'A sniper, aye?' He placed one polished shoe on the mid-step of a stile we had come to so that the crease of his trousers stood out like a bayonet. 'Needs to be a peculiar sort, not one you'd seek out for a pal. Keeps to himself, doesn't say a lot, has the whole thing worked out upstairs. Often uses a building, or a tree, or a belfry. Spends hours up there. Like deer stalking. Knows his man, you see. Knows his man is down there and that his man's name is on the bullet. Knows his man the same way as I know you.'

As clouds parted, the light in the valley leapt extravagantly.

'Have you ever seen one at work?'

'Just heard one. Like the crack of a dry branch. All he needs is half a second. No more.'

My father sat very still, the ash on his cigarette grown long.

'And what does the man who's hit feel?'

He shook his head. 'Just like turning out a light.'

When we went out and met friends, such as the Santrys, the Captain was charming and amusing and behaved as the natural leader of the group. Handsome and urbane, a delightful companion, he was an officer and a man of honour. At home, it was a different story. Some days he stayed in bed with the curtains drawn, or he would rise before dawn and work on the farm beside Danny until they were both exhausted. He was quite a good horseman, but he had never been able to afford a good horse. Sometimes, when I asked him about his business ventures, he would look at me strangely and, in that moment, I saw fear in his face.

In summer, Waterloo was a blessed place, a warm and scent-laden heaven with its own mountain, which we climbed for picnics and from whose high flanks the distant river mouth and the city of Waterford could be seen. Winters were harsh and inhospitable. From October to early May, we were always cold and frequently hungry. No such discomforts existed in Fowler Street, where everyone ate till their bellies bulged, the coal fire blazed for eight months of the year and I could be near my cousin Iggy.

6

DUBLIN

1964

During the week we lived in a three-bedroom house on a terrace in Rathgar, one of those charming houses with tiny railed-off gardens to the front and enough space behind for a lawn and a shed for the lawnmower. Every Friday at around three o'clock we climbed into our Morris Minor and drove down to Waterloo. On Monday morning, we all got up at seven, locked Waterloo and drove for two and a half hours back to Dublin.

My work in the Economic Section of the Department of External Affairs mostly involved the numerous trade treaties and agreements that Ireland was trying to establish or, where treaties already existed, to extend. Trade was vital, as we had belatedly discovered: we had to earn foreign exchange reserves; we could no longer sit like Celtic gnomes, isolated from the world and hoping that our belief in the Virgin birth would see us through.

'Ireland is changing, you know,' I said. 'Becoming less insular. We're putting the past behind us.'

'Dad says we should never have left the Commonwealth,'

Sugar said. 'He says it was like walking out of the best club there is.'

Her father was rector to a tiny and dwindling Church of Ireland congregation in County Carlow. Gentle and conciliatory, Finley Ferguson had been a chaplain in the war, during which he had been struck by shrapnel and lost the use of a lung. He had been nursed by Madeleine, who came from Belfast, and they married during his convalescence. Madeleine was an impatient, ambitious woman, whose husband was no match for her.

'And perhaps he is right,' I said, 'but nations are different to people. Nations follow their own star, which is how Parnell saw it. When your destiny is in your own grasp, you do what you must.'

'Dad sees it in his parish work,' Sugar said. 'There's very little money around. People are poor. They emigrate from this great nation of ours. He says what he sees is heart-breaking.'

'I think, after independence, and the civil war, we were like a wounded bird. We had to curl up and hide for decades in order to rediscover our strength and pride. To rediscover ourselves, really. To heal. That's the process from which we are now trying to emerge.'

Sugar looked at me thoughtfully. 'Incidentally, what are they really like – the people you work with? Do they all hate the British with a passion? Can't say I blame them if they do.'

'They are far cleverer than that. They understand the Brits. It comes from having someone stand on your neck for seven hundred years – you develop a high sense of awareness as to his weight, his change of mood. You know it every time he farts. He, on the other hand, is largely unaware that you exist.'

'How did they ever give you a job? On the face of it, you embody everything they despise.'

'I am the grandson of Pa Kane from Fowler Street, Waterford, never forget. He was a friend of de Valera's. Granddad once lured a British soldier into the back of a shed and cut his throat with a boning knife.'

'Marty, stop!'

'There was a war. Worse things happened, believe me.'

Sugar shuddered. 'At home, Mother was always talking about standards. About how standards are what distinguishes the civilised from the barbaric, about how the standards in the North are entirely lacking here – or, at any rate, in Carlow.'

The Fergusons lived in a modest bungalow with a painfully tidy front garden. The contrast between this paean to self-contained Protestant standards and Waterloo's sprawling untidiness, with our dung-stands and hens and our warren-like interconnecting rooms, must have confirmed to Madeleine, on her sole visit, that her only daughter had made a huge mistake, for she never set foot in Waterloo again.

'She's a filthy snob,' I said.

'That, too.'

'How did she ever produce a sweet girl like you?'

'If it wasn't for Dad, I would have died.' She looked at me. 'You seldom speak of your parents.'

'Do I not?'

'You know you don't.'

'Dad died when I was still at school. Mother remarried, as you know.'

'I'm just sorry I never met her before she became ill.'

My childhood memories had alkalised into a few vital images: walking Waterloo's fields with my father, walking the streets of Waterford with Iggy.

'Do you think that one's religion has a bearing on the standards to which your mother refers? I know she disapproves of Catholics, but how does she feel about the Renaissance? Has she ever been to Florence, for example? Or Rome? Does she think Leonardo da Vinci was a Prod?'

Sugar laughed. 'She probably does.'

We had met in Main, the home of the Santry family, old family friends, at a midsummer party. She was standing to one side, in the lofted entrance hall, by a long, gilt-framed looking glass, hands joined at her waist, chin raised, her fair hair gathered up and clasped to reveal her long smooth neck. She was lovely. Her cornflower-blue eyes gleamed. Her dress, made of grey twinkling stuff, was fastened at her throat and followed the outline of her figure to her toes; but behind, it was scalloped out to reveal her firm back, deliciously. Her bare arms were shining brown, a silver bracelet clasped her wrist and she wore no rings.

The ballroom, reached through an arch scrolled with vines, was floored in wooden tiles that had become loose here and there, so that as we moved into the waltz, it seemed we were accompanied by castanets.

'I'm a bit rusty,' I said, an understatement.

'You're doing brilliantly.' She glided. 'It's vast here, isn't it?'

'They play tennis on the roof.'

'I know, I'm often invited. Do you not play?'

'Never have.'

'Why not?'

'No time, I suppose. Or laziness. But I fish,' I said.

'There's a river at home and it's full of trout this time of year. We catch lots.'

'On a dry fly?'

'To be honest, my father and I put on boots, get into the river with a net and catch them underneath the banks when they're asleep.'

The four-piece band was swaying bravely through its routine.

'I bet you're very good at tennis,' I said.

'Why do you say that?'

'Instinct. Tell me how you do it.'

'I haven't the faintest idea.'

'I doubt that,' I said and allowed my hand to touch the small of her back.

'There's a lot of hard work involved, but it's worth it.'

'Sounds like you're very determined.'

'It's very technical and boring.'

'Then bore me.'

'It's all about learning things like reaching higher – and higher! – in the serve.' She soared from the floor until, for a moment, her nose was level with mine; then sank again. 'And the new double-handed return.'

'You must have started young.'

'Mother made sure of that,' she said with a laugh that suggested she did not think it funny.

'Don't you find it quite stuffy in here?'

'I'm meant to meet someone,' she said. 'He'll be looking for me.'

'Your boyfriend?'

'Well a friend, yes. You may know him. Christopher Chase.'

From the French windows, four steps led down to a terrace facing south. A moon had yet to rise, but starlight was spread in broad washes and the night carried the musk of Norwegian spruce. As we stood at a hedge of beech, through the trees I could see Waterford blinking in the distance. I cupped the match for her cigarette and she dipped to the flame.

'I love this part of the world,' she said as she exhaled smoke. 'People do what they want. Look around you here – everyone is so relaxed. I envy them.'

She was suddenly so sad that my heart lurched for the want of her. A barn owl sank along the black-etched tree line.

'Oh, there's a ship coming in,' she said.

A tiny set of twin fore-and-aft lights was pushing up the far-off estuary.

'Look!'

I turned to her as a meteor from out over the Comeraghs tore through the heavens and plunged into the night where the ocean began, or so it seemed.

'We think it has landed here,' she said, 'and yet they say it all happens millions of miles away.'

'What does it make you think of?'

'Of all the other times in my life I've been out on such a beautiful night. You?'

'Where we come from, where we're going. How stars collide.'

We stood there, in our moment. I could see how each individual hair was swept up into the bundle above her neck, and the tiny race of gold that channelled tightly down between the blades of her shoulders.

I drew her close and she kissed me.

7

WATERFORD

November 1951

From way below our feet cobblestones echoed under the iron shoes of a dray horse being led to one of the Quays' enclosures. A light rain washed down Patrick Street.

Iggy loved danger. He loved pushing situations to the limit, as when he crawled at dead of night into the Gent's bedroom where my uncle was sleeping noisily and drunk, and robbed change from the pockets of his discarded trousers. Iggy used his pen to spatter ink on the unknowing back of the Christian Brother who regularly flogged him, an offence for which, if discovered, he would surely have received an epic thrashing. His resolute indifference to authority made Iggy irresistible. He had me stand guard outside the window of Wise's shop when he went in to steal oranges and sweets. If I saw Mr Wise approaching from the rear of his premises, I would, as instructed, draw my fingers across my throat, like a pirate, upon which signal Iggy would leave the shop at speed. I sometimes imagined us, pistols in our belts, as members of the Flying Squad.

Sometimes he mocked me for the way I spoke, pointing

out that I had an English accent, which made me try to speak like him, but when I did so he scorned my efforts. He had a habit of hacking up saliva and launching globs of spittle across the street, a practice he excelled at and which I instantly began to imitate. He claimed he could piss further than me, but when it became obvious he could not, I curtailed the arc of my flow so as not to upstage him. The day it was announced in Fowler Street that Uncle Ted would marry Mags McGinn, a woman who had inherited a farm in south Armagh, and that Uncle Ted and Iggy would leave Waterford within the year, I hated that woman with all my heart and prayed at night that she would die so that Iggy and I could stay together.

The rain intensified as we walked down Michael Street, across the Apple Market and into Spring Garden Alley. I didn't mind getting wet, and neither did Iggy, whose hair was plastered flat, making his square head seem even more unusual. Earlier he had made off with bullseyes from a shop in the Apple Market where I had distracted the owner with requests for chocolates she did not have. Midway along the Quay, a man with side-whiskers stood in the rain, peering at the rusting hulk of an abandoned trawler. Stanley Kane, my father's younger brother, was got out in a three-piece suit of green-and-amber tweed; gleaming brown boots with good laces doubled around the ankles; a cream-coloured shirt whose tail now impended below the jacket; and a scarlet tie that flashed like a hot poker as he turned and saw us. Iggy shot an orb of glistening spit that landed just short of Uncle Stanley's boot.

'Uncle Stanley, you're to come home now,' he said.

'Look, we have sweets for you.' He produced a bullseye and began to suck it provocatively. 'Yum! This is yummy, Uncle Stanley!'

Uncle Stanley retreated from his prospect of bobbing gulls, churning currents and the tattoo of rain on the grey river. Apart from bringing in coal for the fire in Fowler Street, and doing some minor jobs in the garden for Granny Kane, Stanley's days were spent down here, on the quay, beside the never still river.

'Sweets,' he said and put out his hand.

'Come on!' Iggy said with a nudge to me. 'Come on, Uncle Stanley.'

'Iggy ... ' Uncle Stanley took a step in our direction, hands held out.

'Is your arse clean, Uncle Stanley?' Iggy asked and held up the sweet. 'Say, "My arse is clean," and I'll give you one.'

When Uncle Stanley reached out, Iggy laughed and danced away. My uncle lunged, but his movements were uncoordinated, and he dropped twenty yards behind us, breathing heavily. Every so often, Iggy picked up pebbles and flung them at Uncle Stanley's big troubled face.

'Is he with you?' asked Granny Kane when we came in, and then, when she saw her son, cried, 'Oh, thank God! You're two great boys! Thank God Stanley's home.'

8

WATERFORD

Early December 1951

The night before my parents were due back in Ireland, when we had washed at the tap stand in the yard, Auntie Kate opened the back door and called out.

'Marty! I'm going to wash your hair – come up here!'

'I'd rather not, thanks, Auntie Kate.'

'I didn't ask you what you'd "rather" or not,' she said, copying my accent. 'I said, come up here.'

I had been out helping Uncle Ted and Iggy, delivering coal, and my hair was matted with dust. Auntie Kate's firm, bare arms rippled.

'Take off your shirt.'

As my ears sang and I braced myself on either side of the enamel basin, I prayed that Iggy would not walk in.

'You're a hardy lad, aren't you?'

She pressed me down and poured warm water over my head from a jug. I felt the cold shampoo and heard her screw back the top on the bottle.

'I know you're going to like this,' she said.

Her fingers were in my hair, circling with great

thoroughness as she sudsed me. Her thumbs entered the groove at the base of my neck and the tips of her fingers gently probed my ears. My groin had rushed into tumult. She reached over to work the scalp above my forehead and her elbows rested on my bare shoulders. She had enfolded me from behind, and I could feel her heat on my backside.

'You have a lovely long back,' she said quietly as she rinsed suds from the basin, held my chin in her hand and kissed the nape of my neck.

I could not stand upright, and she knew it. She poured from a second jug and slicked down my hair. I pressed against the hard table edge and she helped me grind gently, her hands cupping my shoulders. As we rocked together, I suddenly went beyond the point of caring. I let out a cry and she pulled me to her in order to prevent me from swooning. I felt her kiss my shoulders.

'Now, that's much better, isn't it?' she murmured and handed me a towel.

That final night, a cold front had moved in and the town was covered in snow. I came downstairs, dizzy with pleasure and confusion, eager to drink in another sight of Auntie Kate, but she was busy cooking and did not appear to notice me.

'Where's Ignatius?' Granny Kane asked. 'Is he not eating?'

'I put his in the oven,' said Uncle Ted between mouthfuls, winking at me. Earlier I had caught a whiff of burnt rubber, which meant that Iggy, or his father, had been using the soldering iron at their workbench.

Uncle Stanley appeared, furtively, dusting snow from

his clothes. As he struggled from his topcoat, he seemed agitated, water puddling at his feet.

'Stanley, go upstairs now and change those clothes,' said Granny Kane.

Uncle Stanley slunk away, drooling midway between glee and terror.

It seemed impossible that I might have forgotten Waterloo, but that evening, snug, well fed and in love, I could easily have imagined that Fowler Street was where I belonged and that the world to which I was returning was a cold illusion. I went down to the garden to await my turn at the toilet shed. The storm had blown through and the town was bathed in bone-white moonlight. My ears picked up a choking sound. Frost pierced me as I made my way down the icy path of the narrow garden. Iggy was squatted next to the buttress wall, beyond which lay a well of darkness.

'Iggy?'

He shivered and sobbed.

'What's wrong?'

'Uncle Stanley ... Uncle Stanley ...'

'What did he do to you?'

Iggy's eyes screwed up and he began to cry again. Behind him, on an ash tree growing crookedly from the wall, one of his kittens had been crucified. The squirming animal's black fur was torn where six-inch nails had been hammered into it.

'Don't tell Daddy, please,' Iggy said.

Never before had I felt quite the same need to protect someone. I ran up to the little shed beneath the back steps and found a claw hammer. The nails, when I got to them, had not been driven straight or deep. Gingerly, I drew them out, first from the hind legs. The tiny creature wriggled, spat and hissed. Iggy pressed his hands to his ears. I covered the thrashing legs with my left hand and drew out the remaining nails. The kitten leapt into the void.

'She's gone!' Iggy cried.

I hunkered down beside him, but when I tried to put my arm around him, to keep him warm, he pushed me away angrily, as if I were somehow to blame for what had happened. We stayed side by side at the end of Granny's garden until the blood on my hands was crusted. Way below, on the moonlit river, a trawler with an orange spinnaker was tacking upstream. The metal wheels of horse drays made their penetrating revolutions. In another country, where I had not yet been, my father's ship was setting sail.

Part II

Part II

GUELPH LINE, CAMPBELLVILLE, ONTARIO

The Recent Past

When they first arrived here, at dead of night, so many years before that she strains to put a number on them, she wanted dawn never to break. The personnel who had travelled with them from RAF Lakenheath had left. Only as night yielded did she fall into a fitful sleep, and then, soon afterwards, she awoke, bereft and terrified. Eventually, she went out to the garden to find her bearings. Although it was still only nine in the morning, the day was searingly hot. Sun bored into her neck, and in a moment her dress was clinging wet.

The swimming pool, an ugly structure raised on scaffolding and accessed by a ladder, brimmed. Sparrows chattered within a large maple and, as she stood in the overwhelming heat, mutely observing the bountiful tree, a cloud of Monarch butterflies swirled past, brilliant as creation.

Over the months that followed, she came to value the seclusion of their new arrangements. Apart from the occasional truck blast, it was always peaceful: the earth that had been scooped out and banked when the house was built acted as a muffler to the traffic up on Guelph Line.

He was a different story. In the early years, he was often restless, and made phone calls to his contact person, telling him or her, as the case was, that he feared he was going mad. The answer was always the same: it is your choice, Mr Price, but you should know that we consider you to be in permanent danger. How great is this danger, he would ask? Well, Sir, they replied, there have been certain reports that concern us, and since your absolute safety is our priority, we strongly recommend, for the moment, that you remain in place.

Two years later, and only after the most almighty set-to, they provided him with a car. At first, it was a novelty. With the security detail trailing behind, he drove her weekly to Milton, or the short distance into Campbellville, or to Niagara on the Lake, where they sat, like ghosts looking in through a window. He soon tired of that and the car is now seldom used.

Any break from their routine is a novelty. For example, the upcoming pension reassessment has been their talking point for weeks. She can tell he is looking forward to meeting the doctor who will come to evaluate him, and that he will insist that this person stays on afterwards for tea.

She remembers some years back, when he took a bad turn and she had him rushed by ambulance into Milton. The casualty doctor's teeth sparkled and the undersides of his hands were vivid pink. '*No-thing wrong with his heart!*' the doctor cried joyfully. '*No-thing at all!*'

1

Waterloo Farm

January 1962

The big triangular field was nailed like a pennant to the throat of the mountain. Flanked by gorse and heather, it fell greenly from its peak in a series of smooth undulations to the lake stream. The races were being run off in conditions of piercing sleet, snow and ice-laden winds as the runners jumped downhill into driving flurries and crossed the fences laid out along the runnel. Twenty-five or thirty cars, as well as Land Rovers and a few tractors, huddled on either side of the short run-in to the winning post. It was a setting of unbelievable discomfort and unqualified affirmation. My Ransom forbears had presided over the local point-to-point in this field since midway through the nineteenth century, and now, while time still allowed, I had resumed the tradition.

The farm had had no water since before Christmas, when frost had cracked the cast-iron pump like an eggshell, and on Saint Stephen's Day Sugar had made it into the labour ward in Waterford just in time. She came

47

home a few days later with a boy and a nurse, and I broke asunder a hundred-year-old wooden threshing machine to keep the stove alight.

'The woman is not used to this,' Sugar had said to me on New Year's Eve, referring to the nurse whose name was Fleming. 'She'll leave.'

'I'll have to drive her home and petrol is scarce, so tell her she can't bloody leave,' I had said.

After school, I had joined the Royal Engineers for three years, been posted to Africa, seen some action, got demobbed in 1961 and then married. Although we had no money, we decided to try and make a go of Waterloo. It was beautiful but there was no living in it, something I should have known from growing up there. Nonetheless, Sugar and I had both been romantic enough to try and defy reality. In summer, I fished and she played tennis; in winter, we hunted, shot, read and rutted, as she had it. Then the child was born and I knew immediately that we could not go on like this. Something had to be done. We had decided to flog the lot for what we could get, up sticks and move to Canada.

Below me, teal skimmed the surface of the streamlet, then soared, pressing tight to the thigh of the mountain. Despite these wretched conditions, I was rather enjoying myself, for it seemed to underline just how apart we were up here in our eyrie.

As the jockeys' silks penetrated the newly thickening snow like the wings of inexplicable butterflies, I plodded down towards Sugar. Nurse Fleming was carrying Emmet, our son, whose nose alone was apparent. She was tougher than Sugar had given her credit for, Miss Fleming, and may even have been enjoying the day. Must have been a decent sort to have stuck to her post out here, I reflected, as I watched her wading through the snow and singing softly to my newborn son.

'The place is looking great, Marty,' said Bobby Gillece.

I had not seen him walking over, his hat pulled low, his ginger moustache snow-laden.

'Or the bit you can see of it,' I said.

Although a Fianna Fáil alderman in Waterford Corporation, Bobby's efforts to go further in politics had not succeeded. He had inherited a bar – Bobby's Bar – in O'Connell Street, where he and Auntie Kate lived.

'Business good?'

'Good enough, good enough.' Bobby had acquired false teeth, but they sometimes wobbled when he spoke. 'The hours are hard, Sundays, bank holidays. Work, work, work. We never go on holidays.'

'The same as a farmer, then.'

'The lads that have it made are sitting above in Dáil Éireann with a mileage allowance and a fat pension. Not that I'll ever see it.'

'You could try again?'

'Nah, fuck them, they had their chance. It's just a pig's trough up there anyway. I'll do my own thing.'

'Time flies, doesn't it? Seems like only yesterday when you were chasing after Auntie Kate in Fowler Street,' I said with a grin.

Bobby looked at me warily. 'Yeah, yeah,' he said. 'I remember you and Iggy, too. Right little gangsters the pair of you.'

I had often wondered about Bobby's marriage to Auntie Kate. They had been together for over a decade, and even though there were no children, everyone hoped there still might be.

'How is Iggy?' I asked, for I knew Bobby kept in touch.

'As well as can be expected. It took him a long time to get over Ted.'

'Of course.'

'Bloody tragedy,' Bobby said. 'It's a police state up there and if you're on the wrong side of it, God help you. He's my godson, you know.'

'I know,' I said as the image of the Flying Squad went through my mind, closely followed by an image I had never seen: of Bobby in the kitchen in Fowler Street, kissing Iggy.

'You should try and meet him. How long has it been?' Bobby asked.

'A long time. Not since we were children. Not since they left Waterford.'

'He'd love to see you, I know he would,' Bobby said. 'He often talks about you.'

'Does he ever come down this way?'

'Never. He's too busy. They live in their own new world up there,' Bobby said.

I wondered when we left for Canada would Sugar and I ever come back to Waterloo, or would we be too tied up in our own new world to ever bother. A flurry of snow briefly doused us.

'Great old place, this,' Bobby said but kept looking to the valley. 'Long may it last.'

His words rang alarm bells in my ears. Perhaps it was my guilt for having decided to sell Waterloo that had attuned my senses, but all at once I knew that he knew, and for that I resented him. As if to confirm my suspicion, Bobby said, 'Inheritance can be hard, Marty.'

'What do you mean?' I asked, knowing my voice was harsh.

'You come into what you didn't ask for, you have to try and keep it on out of a sense of obligation. At the same time, you still have to live your life.'

We tugged our hats even lower and dug deep into the pockets of our coats. Sheep on a hillside half a mile away stood out intermittently like flecks of tin.

'Where will you go?' he asked.

'Canada, perhaps.'

'You'd have contacts there, I suppose.'

'From the army. One chap makes animal feeds out in Western Canada. Says I could be a salesman.'

The snow ceased abruptly and we had sight of a knot of bright colours moving at mid-speed over a starved landscape.

'There's another way too, you know.'

Bobby's teeth wobbled.

'You could get a job in Ireland, hold on to Waterloo,' he said.

'Who the fuck would employ me?'

'Maybe *they* would,' Bobby said and handed me a tear of newspaper.

It would be days before I remembered our discussion, or even looked at the public-sector notice advertising the competition. Frantic shouts could suddenly be heard, and a crowd was running towards the stream. I could see steam rising from behind a brush fence. A mare had slid into the butt and cartwheeled, onlookers said later. The horse had landed with full force on her rider who now lay, motionless, one leg pointing to the sky. What I remember most, though, was the small girl running downhill with hands outstretched to the crumpled heap of silks and crying out, 'Dada! No, please, Dada!'

Three weeks later, I sat in a leather armchair in the first-floor room of a beautiful mansion overlooking St Stephen's Green. The man across from me, in his mid-forties, with raven hair brushed to a flat shine, was called Mr Séamus de Bárra. He had a round, enquiring face and wore spectacles with dark rims. More than a hint of the priest clung to Mr de Bárra. His card said he was a counsellor in the Political Division of the Department of External Affairs.

'You served in the British Army and your father had a good war, Mr Ransom,' he said.

Outside and below, a bicycle bell tinkled.

'I must say, I didn't think such things counted here, especially not in this building,' I said.

'You'd be wrong there. Political decisions are the froth of a moment. When the froth subsides, you're left with the bedrock,' Mr de Bárra said.

'Neutrality in the defining war of the century is a bit more than froth,' I said.

Mr de Bárra smiled thinly. 'I can see how you'd feel that, your father having fought so gallantly, and won, but young nations need to define themselves, particularly where their old neighbours are concerned. We both survived – that's the main thing.' He sat back and regarded me with interest. 'We are a small nation with few resources apart from our people. We have to box clever, Mr Ransom. Times are tough, I don't need to tell you. Go down to the North Wall any night of the week and count the young lads taking the boat-train to Euston.'

'If we'd fought, the American money would be here

now,' I said. 'The young lads might not need to take the boat-train.'

'The great advantage of being alive is that you can live in the present. Leave the past to the dead, Mr Ransom, or to the professors down in Trinity College, is my advice.'

I had a feeling we had met before, which we clearly had not.

'Freedom starts in the blood but it's proven in the pocket. Leaving aside matters such as injustice, criminal misrule and the flagrant and persistent breach of standards long held to be common between civilised peoples, we still have to wake up every day and put food on the table. This can be a problem for a poor island nation, no matter how free. We may have severed our heads from Britain, but not our bellies. We need them, Mr Ransom, now more than ever.'

He crossed his legs and made a delicate gesture with his small hands, like a priest offering a chalice to his congregation. 'You are blessed with unique assets with which to help your country. It will, of course, take time for us to realise that potential, and for the moment we cannot say where your assets will be best invested. We will equip you in whatever way we can, we will give you a good job, a rank and a pension, but we will in no way try to change you. You must continue to be yourself, to live the life you were born into, which includes continuing to own your lovely farm outside Waterford and circulating here and across the water in those circles for which our political status is merely an amusing footnote. You will be their kind of chap, but you will be our chap too – do you get my meaning?'

'Yes, sir,' I said as my ears became full of competing noises.

Mr de Bárra got to his feet. He had grown used to power, I could see, and would never be easily intimidated.

'I have one question. Elementary but necessary.' His unflinching stare. 'What man are you at the end of the day, Mr Ransom?'

I saw in frames of time broken down so small they were immeasurable a boy in short pants trying to heft a sack of coal from a dray. I said, 'An Irishman.'

'I like the way you say that,' chuckled Mr de Bárra and briefly clapped my shoulder as we walked from the room. 'It has style.'

At the foot of the great stairs, we paused at a door, beyond which lay my coat in the care of a porter.

'You will receive an envelope in the next few weeks with all the details. There will be an exam in Dublin, but you'll have no problems. Have you a few words of Irish at all?'

'*Cúpla focail,*' I said.

'That's the spirit,' Mr de Bárra said and extended his hand. 'You'll be very welcome here, Mr Ransom.'

'Marty,' I said with a rush of uplifting hope.

'De Bárra,' said the Counsellor in the Political Division and opened the door.

2

DUBLIN

1965

The Department of External Affairs was run with slender resources, the legacy of successive governments regarding it more or less as a nuisance. My desk overlooked the Iveagh Gardens, in which students from the university walked hand in hand, or sat on benches, or on warm days lay on the grass, puffing cigarettes. As an executive officer, I shared with two others an office adorned with an Adams-style fireplace and fragments of rococo plasterwork on the ceiling. My days were often spent exchanging drafts of proposed treaty clauses with the visiting members of foreign trade delegations. Each evening, the custom was to bring them to dinner in the Russell Hotel, near the office, or to Jammet's at the end of Nassau Street, where Château Mouton Rothschild was usual, the cost of which could only be justified in light of the ultimate trade benefits to Ireland. On those occasional evenings when I was included, I could unfailingly, when I arrived home, transcribe the details of what had been revealed over dinner, and relay them the next morning to the First Secretary in my section, Bill O'Neill.

Bill was a man of few words who seldom allowed the pressure of work to ruffle his demeanour. He smoked a pipe and always wore what appeared to be the same, carefully pressed, pinstriped dark suit. Unmarried, in his late thirties, Bill lived, presumably alone, in a flat off Lower Baggot Street to which no one I knew had ever been invited. His ever-curious expression always made me assume that he knew what I was thinking.

Some weekends, if the weather was particularly foul, and the prospect of opening up Waterloo and trying to heat it too much, I brought Sugar to the races at Leopardstown, just south of Dublin. As we drank hot toddies and watched sodden horses battle it out, I developed a nodding acquaintance with some of the rising men in Ireland, characters who were clever with money, whose politics was Fianna Fáil and who measured their success by their proximity to the Minister for Finance, Charles J. Haughey. One of these men, Bunny Gardener, an accountant who was close to Haughey, was very charming and always made a point of greeting me and Sugar whenever we met. I must have given him my card, for he occasionally sent me complimentary tickets for those race days when, as he put it, the boss would not be needing them.

Mr Haughey often showed up at receptions in Iveagh House, when my role was to wait inside the door and greet visitors, or direct them to the cloakroom. A bantam of a man, his intense blue eyes searched the room over my shoulders. Power oozed from him. The source of his personal wealth, his political ruthlessness, and how he was said to be generous to his friends when it came to sharing market-sensitive information known only to the exchequer, was part of the common gossip. Occasionally, I spotted him at the races, a princely aura to him, moving assuredly with a gaggle of acolytes in his wake.

3

DUBLIN

1966

Sugar said one evening in January, 'You'll never guess who rang today. Christopher Chase.'

'Christopher?'

'Yes, apparently Alison is being sent to work in the embassy here and Christopher's got a job in a merchant bank.'

I felt a little pull of excitement. 'Good for Christopher,' I said.

Over the months that followed, the Chases arrived in Dublin and settled in, and their two daughters found suitable schools. We gave whatever support we could. No plan existed, no formal arrangement. We were just a foursome in our mid-twenties, with Alison the only member who was not Irish, as we sometimes liked to remind her. It was a given that the Chases would spend some weekends with us at Waterloo, where we all hiked, played tennis and caught trout, and that I would show them around the hidden alleys and squares of Waterford. On several occasions, we all drove to County Kerry and spent the weekend with the Chases in their holiday bungalow on Caragh Lake. Alison was Whitehall to her core, but what she did exactly in the British Embassy was never discussed. I came to value the intellectual dimension she brought to our little group, and the scope of her erudition, particularly when it came to English history. To my great delight, she revealed that she was writing an account of the allied advance on the Rhine, which allowed me to dig out my father's papers from 1944, long mouldering in a box, and present them to her.

I threw a party in Waterloo for Sugar's twenty-fourth birthday. All the guests were locals, except for Alison and Christopher. It wasn't until the van from Wise's grocery arrived that Sugar had any clue of what I'd arranged, and then she began to fret that the house was a shambles, and said that I should have painted the place in my spare time, or at least tidied away our stacks of inherited books and pictures, and did we have sufficient plates, glasses and cutlery for twenty people? She was still declaiming as I gathered her up and carried her to our bedroom.

September light curled softly around the lake and danced up the side of the mountain. Michael Small, my mother's husband, danced the Twist with Sugar, and Jack Santry was moved to sing a ballad about fox-hunting that ran to over twenty verses. Later, Bobby Gillece poured his heart out to Sugar, who sat attentively as he described his anguish when he had tried to get the Fianna Fáil nomination for the general election, and failed, she told me afterwards, adding that something about Bobby always gave her the creeps. It was after midnight when the last of our guests drove away. Christopher had gone to bed, wall-eyed, and Sugar, a rug pulled up to her chin, was asleep on the sofa.

'A nightcap,' I said to Alison.

A bench beyond the tennis court overlooked the lake as moonlight rippled in the silky water. Somewhere, way out behind the wall of darkness, the rasp of a fox gave notice that she was on the move.

'How lovely it is here,' Alison said.

'We are the lucky beneficiaries of someone else's foresight.'

'That gets lost sometimes,' she said, 'the fact that we are often just carriers, part of a line, or a team. Like a relay race.'

'I know,' I said and felt my heart skip.

'You've been passed the baton, Marty. It's up to you whether or not you want to take it and keep going.'

'Are you sure we should be having this conversation?'

'You are very much part of a tradition, one that is old and honourable.'

'Oh, come on! We're just hill farmers!'

'You know what I mean. I can help you keep that tradition going.'

My blood must have suddenly warmed, for I felt it rush into my neck and groin with a sudden blot of happiness.

'You are ideally placed,' she said. 'What is more, the kind of relationship I propose is exactly what your superiors in Dublin would expect of someone in your position. There is nothing wrong in such an arrangement. On the contrary, it is honest and upright since only good can come to both sides from it.'

The moon had come to a point where the shoulder of our mountain would shortly devour it.

'I do of course understand how such a proposal may not suit you, and how you will need to reflect before you decide. Neither is there any urgency required. In fact, my advice is that you take as much time as you need to make up your mind, since decisions of this kind have to be made alone.'

'I'm a freak,' I said. 'I don't belong to one side or the other.'

'It is the world around you that is freakish. You and I, on the other hand, know what it is to hold the longer view. We live in an era full of contradictions, where chaos is the only certain outcome. You can be a bulwark against that chaos, those contradictions.'

I could have breathed in the scents of the dying summer and slept for ever.

'They'll hate me,' I said.

'You'll be doing the honourable thing,' she said. 'Don't ever let anyone tell you otherwise.'

I made no decision, but swayed for months in a cross-breeze of indecision, perhaps lacking the courage to admit what I really was. Entranced by the prospect Alison had held out to me, yet terrified by my own potential, I decided to put distance between us, to give myself time to think. When we were invited to the Chases' Halloween party, I invented a reason why I could not accept. Then, just before Christmas, when some small concessions were suddenly made by the British in an aspect of trades and tariffs in which I was directly involved, Bill O'Neill called me in and told me that I was to be promoted to higher executive officer, which meant that my salary would be increased. When I came home and told Sugar, she jumped into my arms, wrapped her legs around my waist and hugged me.

4

LONDON

Spring 1967

Our embassy was located in a decent house on Grosvenor Place and overlooked Buckingham Palace Gardens, a detail that always raised a smile, on the first telling. An important trade memorandum between Ireland and the United Kingdom was dragging its way to a conclusion and, because of my experience, Bill O'Neill had sent me over to help out. After Séamus De Bárra's sudden death the year before, Bill had been promoted to the Political Division as Counsellor and had taken me with him. Bill was the man who liaised, from time to time, on behalf of the department, with the intelligence sections of both the Garda Siochána and the army, although with whom he liaised, or about what, was never discussed.

The Naval & Military Club, on Piccadilly, known also as the In & Out, was where my father had once been a member. The porter, Hobson, recalled him.

'Remember the Captain very well, sir. Liked a little flutter, as I'm sure you know. Knew his form, Captain Ransom.'

Hobson's glass-fronted cubicle occupied a corner of the spacious hall, at the Piccadilly entrance, and looked out on Green Park. A coal fire blazed beneath a grand portrait of the monarch. Hobson had apparently served as an orderly during the war and had been decorated. With a head of persistent blond curls, he was a man for whom nothing was impossible if it involved him receiving a ten-shilling note. I breakfasted every morning in the dining room, beside the inner courtyard with its pool in which ornamental carp thrashed among lily pads. On rainy days, the Underground brought me to Hyde Park Corner where I surfaced amid the extensive statuary associated with Wellington.

My mission entailed the sort of endless redrafting with which I had become familiar, the scrambling for position, the tireless appraisal of the effects of our decisions on third countries, and the stamp of our legal people on every paragraph. Still, it was exciting to be in London, where a sense of power, lacking utterly in Dublin, made me yearn to somehow be part of it but at the same time to remain as I was. In the evening, when I sat in what was known in the club as the ladies' bar, with its door to Half Moon Street, its chintz couches and the daily newspapers correctly arranged, I felt a sense of homecoming that both comforted and surprised me. One of my counterparts in Whitehall contacted me during the first week and took me to dinner in Soho, after which we went on to a night-club where we both got drunk. In the days that followed I made contact with friends who had been fellow-officers, but, apart from one invitation to supper in Cheyne Walk, all the others were either away, or if not, promised to call me back, which they never did.

One day, I left the embassy at lunchtime and made my way to Somerset House on the Strand, where the details of all deaths in the UK since 1937 were stored and indexed. I expected to find the entry quite handily, but that evening, when I was the last member of the public remaining, I had still not found what I was searching for. Perplexed, I returned a few days later, and searched again, but the outcome was no different.

At the beginning of the following week, I was included in a birthday luncheon at a restaurant in Knightsbridge, which ended with no one returning to the embassy, circumstances that I gathered were not unusual. Later, at the club, I was seized by a deep yearning that had waited more than six months for its moment, but which, now that it had arrived, had to be answered. I went to the coin-box by the lift and dialled the number. It was answered on the second ring.

'Alison Chase,' she said.

5

LONDON

Spring 1967

She was brief, asking me where I was staying, and for how long. Something in her manner, or tone, which was efficient and business-like, made me immediately regret the call, as if I had handed over something I could not get back, or had misinterpreted what she had said to me that night by the lake or as if the drink of earlier had made a fool of me.

A week later, after a long meeting on the second floor of the embassy, where a trade delegation from Canada was being entertained, I left in the dark and, despite the rain, decided to walk back to the In & Out. Buses sloshed surface water on to the pavement opposite Old Park Lane. I crossed to Green Park, with its scent of cut grass, and then jay-walked back across the wide thoroughfare to the front entrance of the club where I arrived soaked and dripping in front of Hobson.

'Let me take your things, sir. I'll hang them downstairs beside the boiler. Be dry as toast in a jiffy.'

He took my hat, mac, scarf, gloves and umbrella. I was looking forward to an evening with a drink after dinner, the newspapers, and, if there was anything worth seeing, an hour at the new colour television that had been installed in the ladies' bar. I was beginning to forget my telephone conversation with Alison.

'And a letter for you, sir.'

'Really?'

'Hand-delivered before lunch,' Hobson said.

The train sped by way of industrial locations, past huddled roofs of weeping smoke, by upstairs windows with curtains drawn unevenly. Mongrels shook out bags of rubbish in the spectral post-dawn. Occasionally, we passed water-filled craters in the midst of terraces where the bomb damage of more than twenty years earlier had yet to be redressed. In rain, I disembarked at Watford, as instructed. Outside the station, the lights of an Austin Cambridge flashed. I peered inside it, expecting to see Alison, but a man half my size with a military haircut got out and held open the back door.

'Is Alison... ? Mrs Chase ...is she... ?'

'I expect so, sir,' he said cheerfully as I climbed in.

The last of the suburbs gave way to vales and shires where cattle huddled along dripping hedgerows and dark blankets of crows rose and fell over the terrain. After thirty minutes, in pounding rain, we turned into an open gateway and drove up an avenue between white iron railings, the sort you might expect in a nursing home. A gravel sweep washed up to a porch. Did Alison work here when she was in England? The front door was opened. A large man stood there, smiling crookedly, face animated. His wad of russet hair was crisp and crinkly and he wore a navy bowtie with white spots.

'Hello, chum.'

I stared at him. 'Good God! Vance!'

6

SAINT LAWRENCE ABBEY SCHOOL, SHROPSHIRE

February 1953

Some nights, I preferred to go out alone and wade through snow drifts rather than spend another long evening huddled at the outer rim of the great fire. I trudged up behind the castle, imagining myself on Waterloo farm, and probed the hedgerows with the light beam of a torch to make out the yellow eyes of the Welsh ewes clustered there. Their completeness comforted me. I yearned for a fleece to warm me in freezing England, to sleep in the penetrating air, to smell the dung of animals. I longed to be Iggy, and at home with my dad.

We were served our meals in three separate locations: juniors, such as me, in a warm room beside the kitchen; intermediates in a large, cold, rectangular hall with enormous paintings depicting boars being hunted and killed; and the senior boys in a freezing circular tower that was also the school library. Dom Nestor, Saint Lawrence's headmaster, his hands twisted into bulbous, arthritic knuckles, presided at the high table. Known as Nessie, he had one eye pupil locked into the bottom of its socket, his nose dripped, and his Adam's apple protruded almost level with his chin. We ate the estate's mutton, as a rule, but every other week the brother in charge of the farm killed a pig.

After supper and before second study, all sixty of us knelt in the playroom and Nessie led us through the rosary. Unlike the boys from London or Manchester, I was unaffected by isolation. Some, like Welch, and Belclare, the son of a baronet, spent hours planning to run away, although, as I pointed out, since the school lay in a mountain range ten miles from a town, a run-away in such weather would soon perish. We attended the main mass every morning, a mandatory duty, except that junior boys were also on a rota as altar boys, serving the monks in the church's side altars.

I was instructed in such duties by Vance, a prefect several classes above me. His father worked in the diplomatic corps and they lived in Belgium, he told me.

'Mother is an alcoholic,' he said as he pointed vaguely to where the soutanes hung. 'She's having an affair with an Italian diplomat.' It was as if he was describing something he had come across in a book. 'The old man hates her, of course, but one has to keep up appearances. If they weren't bloody Catholics, they'd have divorced. What does your father do?'

'A landowner.'

'Oh, really? How much?'

'We've never really counted.'

'My old man got a bullet in the crotch during the war.'

'My dad shot Germans.'

'They all say that.'

'No, mine did. Twenty in one go. Then he went off and played a round of golf.'

'My father shot a man in Singapore. Through the left eye.'

'Killed him?'

'Left eye, chum, in here and out here. Bloody big hole. Course he killed him.'

'He had a reason, I take it.'

'He was in bed with this chap's wife and the bugger came home and found them. Had to shoot his way out. Do you believe in the afterlife?'

'I'm not sure. I think so.'

'All this nonsense they stuff down our throats here, mumbo bloody jumbo, if you ask me. We live, we eat, we fornicate, we die. So how about your old lady? Anyone else in her knickers?'

'Sorry?'

Vance smiled as if I was slow on the uptake. 'They all do it, you know.'

I swallowed. 'What?'

'Come on, Ransom! They're like bunnies, after only one thing. You ever fucked one?'

'No,' I said, wishing I had paid more attention to Danny's descriptions behind the pigsty in Waterloo.

'Me neither, but I'm hoping to this Christmas. The chauffeur is bringing me to a brothel. Ah well, look, this mass thing is like falling off a log. Who are you serving?'

'Father John.'

'Ah. Hates it if you're not quick up with his wine, or if you put in too much bloody water. Queer as a blind drake, of course, but so are they all, let's be honest. But you're probably safe given your size. They like smaller chaps, like what's his name in your class? Blond hair?'

'Belclare?'

'Is that his name? You can bet he's had a rumble from one of them. Come to think of it, I wouldn't mind giving him a length myself. Don't have any cigarettes, do you?'

My father never wrote to me, but my mother did. Her letters came every week and told me of the day-to-day life in Waterloo, of how well my pony was doing, of the hunt the previous week, during which the fox had run a straight line for five miles from Ballyhale, and how they were all looking forward to me coming home for Easter. Each week I climbed to a combe in the hills behind the abbey with her letter and read it over and over.

'Ireland remains a discontented province of the Empire,' proclaimed Dom Alfred, a man of wobbly jowls who had written books on history. 'It is to be hoped that someday she will appreciate the favours that have been graciously bestowed on her and will play her part in the great family of British nations. Yes, Ransom?'

'Ireland is a Republic, father, not a province of the Empire.'

'I was using a figure of speech, you odious child. A small and poor country such as Ireland will always have to rely on her larger neighbour to survive, one way or t'other. It is to England's credit that she has not cut Ireland adrift.'

Welch, sitting directly behind me, stuck his toe into my back and kicked. Sniggers encouraged Dom Alfred to continue.

'We are in the middle of an unprecedented geopolitical crisis in which solidarity between the nations of the West means that the idea of neutrality, as proclaimed by little Ireland in the last war, is the tactic of fools. In the face of the Soviet threat, Irishmen, too, will have to fight if we are to be spared from this new evil.'

'The fact that Ireland was neutral, father, does not mean that Irishmen did not fight,' I said. 'My father fought, for example.'

'Good for him.'

'And my grandfather – in the Highland Brigade.'

'The Boer War, indeed. Fought to hold sway over the blackamoor. You think the blackamoor is fit to govern himself? Ask your grandfather. Then ask him what he thinks about the Irish.'

'My grandfather is dead.'

'Nonetheless.'

'The Irish fought the British and won their independence,' I heard myself say.

'Some prize indeed,' said Dom Alfred, slyly. 'Twenty-three per cent of the world's population look to Westminster for governance but brave little Ireland knows better. By the way, Ransom, why have you been sent here for your schooling and not to a pigsty in Eire?'

General laughter brought victory to the priest's cheeks as Welch kicked again, harder, and I felt a surge of fierce loyalty.

'I'm sorry, Ransom? No Irish school suitable, was there?'

'My family have always been educated in England. It is our tradition. I was merely pointing out a matter of fact.'

'And the matter of fact I was making is that a bog will scarcely be enough to feed a nation, even one as used to muck as Eire,' said Dom Alfred to applause, as the door opened. 'What?'

Vance stood there in his sports coat and grey flannels, looking furtive.

'Excuse me, Father.'

'Yes, what is it, Vance?'

'Father Nestor wishes to see Ransom,' Vance said.

A winding corridor linked the classrooms to the castle, through a room where our shoes were kept on numbered shelves, by way of the urinals, and led to a flight of stairs laid down in cold brown marble.

'What's he want me for?' I asked again.

'Told you, haven't the remotest, old boy,' Vance said breezily, although his replies came tinged with a quality of evasion that unsettled me.

I already smoked quite heavily, and the middle finger of my right hand was tobacco-stained, something Father John had remarked on with displeasure when I had last served him at mass.

'Has Father John complained about me?'

Smoking was an offence for which I had already been given detention; repeated convictions resulted in flogging, a punishment I was familiar with and whose execution Nessie reserved to himself.

'It's smoking, isn't it?' I asked as we arrived outside an oak door set into a deep, stone wall.

'It's not smoking, chum,' said Vance with a little grimace as he pressed the bell, stood back and, with an almost courtly gesture, indicated that I should enter.

Father Nestor's study was furnished with a narrow bed, a wash basin, a gas ring with a kettle, an armchair, and a desk frothing with opened books and sundry papers. My previous visits here had involved me lowering my trousers and drawers and leaning forward across the armchair as Nessie had flogged my arse with a bamboo cane.

'Ah, Ransom, come in and sit down, please.'

Drips fell from Nessie's nose, his demon eye watered and his Adam's apple leapt.

'Martin,' he said with a frown and consulted a file lying open in front of him. 'It is Martin?'

'Yes, Father.'

'It's just that some chaps don't answer to their christening appendage.' He wiped his nose with a rag and cleared his throat. 'Martin, the dear Lord has never given us explanations for His decisions, and we, His little children, are left to trust in His infinite wisdom, which in turn is informed by His love for each and every one of us. It is not our place to question His will, but to accept it, however painful that may be. What do we know of His great design? Almost nothing. Were we, mere children, present at the birth of creation? No, we were not. And even had we been, what could we have contributed to that cosmic drama? Would we have had the vision that saw fish evolving into popes and kings? That saw mice begin their long journey to become the Woolly Mammoth? Not likely, but the Lord did. He is all-knowing, all-wise, all-loving and all-merciful. Happy are we who are called to His table.'

Amid this mangled excursion through Nessie's justification of his own irrelevance came the ominous sound of danger and my ears began to hum.

'We are born, we die. Life is but a preparatory stage for the great celebration that awaits us in heaven, that is, awaits those of us who live and serve the Lord. *Death where is thy sting?* Saint Paul asks in his letter to the Corinthians. Death is nothing, ah, Martin, death is a temporary separation; indeed, death may be embraced fondly as we stumble forward in this life of hard knocks and bumps.'

Unable to contain my terror, I sprang up.

'What?' I cried.

'My poor boy,' said Dom Nestor, his expression that of someone utterly lost, 'your dear father is dead.'

For the remainder of that wretched day, during which I was excused classes and study, Vance never left my side. When I walked from Nessie's room, weak, shaking and disbelieving, Vance was there.

'You knew,' I said.

'I'm afraid so, chum, yes.'

Most of the headmaster's rambling account had escaped me, except for a few essential details: my father had dropped dead in Green Park, not far from his club; cause of death was a heart attack. He had already been cremated. I had not even known he was in London.

In the woods of Lawrence Abbey, in a draughty hut, Vance produced a packet of Players. The taste of that tobacco, before we lit up, and the first, vital suck of smoke, remains for me the last connection to the Captain. Vance and I sat unspeaking, until, eventually, as if we had been immersed in a discussion, he said, 'Sounds like he was a really first-class man.'

'He was more than first class,' I began, as I tried to explain the person I had been so intimately observing and imitating for most of my thirteen years. A man never

entirely at ease, but nearest to being happy at night when
we were all inside, doors locked, shutters barred. In his
mind's eye he was forever fixed on some scheme or other
that would spring him from whatever latest mess he had
slid into. He never truly knew what it was like to live,
other than to be in perpetual flight, urging himself ever
faster to outrun his memories, to launch himself into
fresh schemes, and more trouble, as if to obliterate his
failures that rolled ever larger behind him.

'I hope he didn't suffer,' I said.

'Of course he didn't,' Vance said. 'Heart attack?
Happens the whole time. They feel nothing. Take my
word for it.'

I had studied every one of the Captain's movements:
the way he lit his cigarette, how he arched one eyebrow as
the first response to a question, and how, when he sat on
a wall, or a gate, he brought up his right foot and rested it
on his left knee. I recalled how the darkening pomade he
put in his hair smelled vaguely like saddle leather. I told
Vance about the different voices he used with different
people: how he took on a bit of Danny's accent with
Danny; his swift changes between being happy and stern
when he spoke to Oscar, my dog; and how, with just the
two of us on the mountain, he would sometimes throw
back his head and open his mouth to release a prolonged
roar of joy.

Vance listened with polite interest as I described how
the Captain, when I asked him what he did when he went
away, always became vague. Yet he had spoken warmly
of London, and of the great buildings we would one day
visit together, and trains that ran underground, and of his
club on Piccadilly where he had met the men who ran the

empire. The Captain had spoken of balmy Green Park, and Greenwich, which was the time centre of the world, and Harrods, and London taxis, and told me how one day we would go to Royal Ascot together. It was as if he had wanted to imbue me with something that he feared he might lose, or had already lost, as if I were the one to carry forward the precious memories, as if he knew, even as he was making such promises, that these were promises he would never keep. Our discussions happened when just the two of us were out walking the land, Oscar romping ahead and starting rabbits, the warmth of the sun radiating from the stones in the walls that marked our farm's uneven divisions. On a clear day, when one could just about see, or perhaps, imagine, the Suir, at such moments, the sense that we in Waterloo were not only safe but somehow anointed was something my father relished, I told Vance.

When it grew too chilly, we walked into the hills behind the castle, and I explained, as my tears began, how the truth was that my education was being paid for by my mother's godmother, Auntie Hazel, and that money was a constant source of worry for my father. With his British military title and accent, his larger than life personality and air of entitlement, he had managed all his life to be given credit by bookmakers, hotels, department stores and wine merchants. 'And yet, I once saw him give a pound note to a beggar,' I said. 'A fortune. I asked him why he'd done it and he told me that he wanted to go to heaven when he died.'

'And I'm sure he has, chum,' said Vance with great seriousness. 'Without the slightest doubt, that's where your old man has gone.'

I wept openly, unashamed, as all my memories of the Captain came tumbling out, including how he claimed he had taken ninety Germans prisoner on the Rhine and then driven into German-held Düsseldorf for a beer, and how he'd got wounded in the backside in a house outside Antwerp where he'd been in bed with a nurse when the roof came in. Without warning, Vance began to laugh, and to my surprise, so did I, my tears of desolation turning to fierce, defiant pride, as if we were two brothers for that small window of time.

7

Spring 1967

In a long, book-filled study where a tray with a whisky decanter and tumblers was set out before a fire of aromatic beech, table lights with green shades glowed. Beyond the tall windows I could make out brooding parkland.

'Is Alison here?'

'Couldn't make it, old boy, but sends her warmest regards.' I remembered the big, hooked nose and the feathery eyelashes, except that now they belonged to a rather thickset man. 'Goodness, I often think about the old days! How on earth were we educated – eh? All those bloody monks, queer as tuppenny bits. Still, it was the best my parents could afford at the time.'

We raised our glasses.

'Your father was a diplomat,' I said.

Vance frowned. 'No, I think you must have the wrong chap. My old man worked for a chartered accountant.'

'I'm sorry, I thought he worked abroad.'

'Never left London in his entire life, but sent me to school in Shropshire, as you know.'

'I must be thinking of someone else,' I said as the past scurried through my mind.

'Alison tells me you live on an absolutely gorgeous estate in Ireland,' Vance was saying. 'Mountains, lakes. A beautiful wife, a baby and another expected. A paying job in Dublin. Well done, chum!'

'What about you?'

'Two boys,' he said with a little smile. 'We live in Suffolk and I spend three nights a week in London. Our lads will go to the local grammar, can't afford otherwise. The tax in this country is a real bummer, take my word for it.'

After school, he had joined the RAF and had been posted to a base in Kent, where an unexploded German bomb had gone off one night outside the officers' mess and shattered his eardrum, he told me. 'Been behind a desk ever since.'

'What do you do, Vance?'

'I suppose you could say I keep in touch with certain people,' he replied genially. 'Listen to them with my good ear, so to speak. Provide a link, if you know what I mean. Try to use what I hear to smooth things out, to make sense from nonsense, to occasionally stop people making fools of themselves. Get around the bloody mountains of paperwork. I'm a very small cog in a very big wheel.'

'Foreign Office.'

'Well, yes, exactly. Full of the most boring old farts who've been there since the Flood, celluloid collars and bowlers, wandering around dreaming of gin, some of them have spent their lives in Burma, or Ceylon, or Hong Kong. We're just nannying them, basically, until it's time for them to go home and die. But I expect you have them too.'

'I work as a higher executive officer in the political division of External Affairs,' I said. 'Sometimes it's like watching paint dry.'

'But you at least had a bit of excitement after school, from what I hear.'

'It wasn't all that much, believe me.'

He offered cigarettes from a sandalwood-lined box. 'What regiment?'

'Royal Engineers.'

'Ah, the good old sappers!'

'A mere probationary second lieutenant, I'm afraid. Africa.'

'The dark continent,' Vance said. 'If you ask me, we'll be damn lucky to get out of it.'

'I was in charge of a military survey team, three hundred miles south-west of Nairobi. One night, the Mau Mau ambushed me when I was out having a piss, shot and ate my horse and then tried to hold me hostage.'

Vance's eyes shone with admiration. 'But you made a run for it.'

'After ten days, when it was touch and go whether I'd be next on the menu. Walked for five days,' I said. 'I was rescued by some Maasai.'

'And now we have all your chaps' maps to show for it, but no bloody country.' He leaned back and joined his hands. 'History is a bugger, isn't it? A small island like ours, by virtue of philosophy, brains, guts and vision manages to take over half the bloody world. I mean, look at what the Venetians achieved – all they owned was a sodding swamp and yet they controlled the Mediterranean. However, one has to believe in something, so for me that something is what we still have and are trying

81

to hold on to. A way of life, things I dare say you under-stand, chum.'

'England's record is poor when it comes to Ireland.'

'"Poor" is kind – I would say appalling. Which is a very good reason for wanting to correct the balance. We have no huge expectations that matters in Ulster will ever be other than bloody awful. The way they rig the voting and stack their police force with Unionists. Sooner or later it's going to come back to bite them. Our wish would be to contain the thing when it blows up. To at least know what's going on.'

'You think it will blow up?'

'We play second fiddle in this to our friends in the Special Branch of the Met, who've been hunting down Fenians for a hundred years. But bad government – and Ulster's is the worst kind – always blows up eventually. And here's the thing, chum: you never know where it might end. Could well spill across the border and swallow up you chaps. Which is the last thing anybody wants, I think you'll agree. The problem is, if that does happen, we don't think you lot have, shall we say, the resources to contain it. We think you'll need some help.'

'What kind of help?'

Vance got to his feet and grimaced as he stretched his back. 'What we have in mind is friendly awareness. Uncle and nephew is far too patronising, but you get the drift. A way of sharing common thoughts and concerns. A way of making what's blocked, fluid. Both sides working in each other's best interests.'

He was pacing down to the book-lined far wall, and back again, swinging his arms.

'So, we might ask you, chum, what exactly is the

thinking regarding such-and-such – off the record, of course – and you might say, well, our chaps can't get anywhere with, whomever, in Ulster, and we might say, well, we're paying the fat bastard's salary, why don't you let us give him a little nudge, eh? And that's it really. You may not always know the answers, of course, but your ministry, if you'll permit me to say so, is on the small side, and therefore information is probably more shared than not. Look, no one expects hundreds of years of history to dissolve over a wet weekend, but at least if we can help each other informally, then surely that's the least we should do?' Vance looked suddenly at his wrist-watch as if he had just remembered another appointment. 'But I mustn't keep you; you've already been more than generous with your time.'

'I've taken the day off,' I said.

'The least you deserve,' he said as we walked towards the hall and I heard the car outside starting up.

'Vance.'

His crooked grin. 'Old boy?'

'There is one thing.' I drew him into an alcove beside the hall door. He nodded as I spoke and his fixed regard never left my face. 'I've searched extensively, but I can't seem to find a record of it,' I concluded.

'Not a problem,' Vance said. 'Happy to try and help, chum.'

'Are you sure? I mean, I'm not trying to take advantage...'

'Nonsense! What are friends for?' he asked as we resumed our progress towards the car.

It had stopped raining and I could now see ancient trees in the nearby paddocks.

Vance said: 'Further to what we've just discussed, you'll find some small concessions from Whitehall that should go down well. Important that your career be a success. And of course, regarding today, just pull the ladder up behind you, what?'

'Understood.'

'Excellent, excellent.'

'So…how do we…converse?' I asked.

Vance laughed. 'As simply as possible, please God. My word, what a bloody day. I fantasise at times like these of being in the South of France, but of course I'll never be able to afford it.'

8

PARIS

April 1969

Spring blossom scents skirmished with those of French tobacco and high octane gasoline. Waiters in green aprons brushed out their cafés and restaurants. On an impulse, I purchased, for the equivalent of nearly ten pounds, a swooping panama with a black band from the millinery establishment of Motsch Fils & Cie on the Avenue George V.

'You look splendid!' Sugar said.

I loved the way she drew men's glances, how her neck arched when she turned to me, her reflection in the windows of shops and parked cars, which sometimes made me look twice, as if I had just seen her for the first time. We lunched in Fouquet's, on asparagus and artichokes, a veal chop and a piece of sole. A bottle of Montrachet. Something utterly affirming about sitting on one side of a white-clothed table, looking out over boxes of geraniums at the spinning world.

Nothing had really happened. I occasionally asked

myself if the Vance I had met in Hertfordshire was the same Vance I had known in school, and whether he and I were really now on the one side of an enterprise whose objectives were, to put it mildly, hazy. Alison certainly never referred to him. Nor did she ever probe me for information, or offer any from her side, or set me a task or make a suggestion as to a course of action she felt would benefit Ireland, even when I described for her the difficulties I was running up against with the Brits, albeit at a level where only minnows toiled. On the other hand, I was gaining a reputation for achieving results, however minor. On more than one occasion, Bill had given me a job with the words, 'Marty, you'll understand how best Whitehall will react to this one.'

We swung over the Seine, the taxi's windows down, and drove out through the Bois. I can see it now! At the racecourse in Saint-Cloud tables were set out on the lawn with buckets for champagne. So bloody civilised! We made our way by merry flowerbeds as horses and jockeys flashed by on their way to the beginning of a race. It was wonderful. Just the place to start a little civil war.

'Where on earth are we going?'

I steered Sugar down steep steps beneath skull and crossbones on a sign saying 'Passage Interdit!' We went blind coming in from the daylight. It was a basement service area, beneath the grandstand, with boilers, cellars, stacked crates of beer and further storage vaults for vegetables. Pipes ran along the ceiling inches from my head. At a counter, a barman in a white jacket was serving champagne. Although I had observed Mr Haughey at Leopardstown, and had taken his coat at receptions in

Iveagh House, we had never had a conversation. Of lesser build to me, but compact and fit, with slicked dark hair and hooded eyes, he stepped forward from the group he was drinking with.

'At last, the sunshine.' He kissed Sugar's hand. 'And of course, Mr Ransom.'

He made a fuss of getting Sugar a drink, hand to her bare elbow. She said later that, although she had been predisposed to dislike him because of his reputation, she found herself instantly revising her opinion. Haughey picked up glasses and a bottle and beckoned me to a corner where, for some reason, there stood an upright piano.

'Mr Ransom.'

'Minister.'

We touched glasses.

'The boss man used to come down here. Sent runners upstairs with his bets. Five hundred francs, on the nose, every race. No one could see him down here. Private.'

'It certainly is that, Minister.'

He looked at me sideways as he heard my accent. 'Bunny was right. You're the real McCoy, aren't you? Very clever, very clever indeed. And now with the grade of higher executive officer.'

Our airline tickets and our hotel had all been prepaid, and then conveyed to me by Bunny Gardener, the accountant who seemed to be involved with Haughey at every level, even though Gardener was a businessman with no elected function.

Haughey smiled. 'Your wife is very attractive.'

'Her first time here.'

'Ah, I love it. I love horses: the smell of them, the power

of them. I ride out every day, you know.' He poured champagne. 'This problem at home.' He smacked his lips. 'You know what I'm referring to?'

I nodded cautiously.

His eyes swivelled. 'It will probably get worse. It's getting ugly.'

Eruptions of laughter sang along the pipes. An old porter appeared, wheezing through with a trolley of stacked crates.

'They need help,' Haughey continued when the man had gone by. 'For their self-defence. They have a right to defend themselves; everyone has. When the civil rights marchers were ambushed at Burntollet Bridge the RUC didn't lift a fucking finger to help them.'

'I know, Minister.'

'So they need the means of self-defence.'

'Naturally.'

'This new crowd don't give a fuck for tradition, or what the old fools who've led them to this point think. They're going to split, you know.'

'I had heard as much suggested, yes, Minister.'

'I want you to make contact on my behalf. Unofficially.'

'Minister?'

'Through your cousin, Ignatius Kane.'

It was as if he had struck me in the chest. I may even have taken a step back.

'I wasn't aware that ... Iggy Kane? You mean that he is ...?'

'You look as if you've seen a fucking ghost, Ransom. For Christ's sake, this is very simple. Kane is active; he's one of the new crowd. You're his first cousin. I want you to give him a message. What part of all that do you not understand?'

I was reeling, but at the same time trying to work out how he had come by this information. 'Iggy Kane and I haven't met in many years, sir. I'm not sure that—'

'It will be a personal favour to me, of course, without reference to anyone in your department. You're Political Division. Who do you report to in there?'

'Bill O'Neill, Minister.'

'O'Neill. I know him. Inquisitive type. Likes to talk the republican talk, but you never know with fucking civil servants.' Haughey looked at me steadily. 'There's cash available, plenty of it. I want Kane to be told and to pass the message up.'

'Of course I can try to contact him, sir, but ….'

Haughey's expression brimmed with disdain.

'Well, Minister, he and I have lost touch, and for all I know his alleged associates may not wish to be helped in the fashion you describe.'

'Alleged associates? Who do you think you're speaking to? Some fart of a district court judge?'

'I'm sorry, sir.'

'Of course his associates will wish to be helped in the fashion I describe, Ransom. Who else is going to fucking help them?'

'I don't know, Minister.'

'You can say that again.' He scribbled on his race sheet and tore off the corner of it. 'Don't waste time. Have them call me on this number.'

'Yes, Minister.'

He looked at me, shook his head as if disappointment with subordinates was no surprise to him, took up the bottle and walked back towards the counter. Halting, he pivoted. 'By the way, Ransom—'

'Minister?'

'At least you got the hat right.'

Out on the lawn, the trays being carried at shoulder height by perspiring waiters seemed, from a distance, like enormous epaulettes. I very badly needed a drink.

'I spotted a ladies' room,' Sugar said.

'I'll order a Pimm's for you,' I said.

Her figure in blue silk as she moved away, her straight back giving her the appearance of a much taller woman, her lovely fair hair and the swoop of her neck gave me the strength I needed. I was shown to our table and ordered the Pimm's, and a large cognac.

'You're a very lucky man.' I didn't have to turn around. 'But, of course, you don't need me to tell you that, chum.'

He was seated to one side, eating the plat du jour, drinking a half carafe of Burgundy by the look of it. Sunlight glinted on the ridges of his hair. 'Back any winners?' he asked.

'I don't know. Perhaps.'

I could hear his plate being removed as he ordered the chocolate mousse. 'Isn't this just splendid? Has there ever been such an enlightened country? We should bring our children here.'

'When they're slightly older perhaps.'

He chuckled. 'How old is Emmet now? Six?'

'Nearly eight. And our baby Georgie is three months.'

'Goodness, how time flies. I shall bring my boys here, before they get too old, you know? Before they get cynical. Like me. Like you, too. Isn't that what we want for them?'

Beyond a hedge, men in bowlers, like figures in a Degas canvas, conferred gravely around a steaming horse.

'It's outrageous,' I said. 'He wants to give money to the new activists through my cousin Iggy Kane, someone I haven't met for twenty years. I didn't even know that Kane was connected to the movement. Haughey wants Kane's people to know that he can provide means for their self-defence. Hard cash.'

'Much?'

'No figure was mentioned, but I was given to understand that there would be enough.'

'Well, he is the minister for finance.' He was laughing softly as his chocolate mousse arrived.

'He's expecting the situation up there to get much worse before too long – something that you alerted me to several years ago, Vance. Congratulations.'

'I'm just an ordinary Joe Soap, Marty, doing his bit for Her Majesty's government. God forbid I should ever be singled out for praise.'

He had not changed one iota from our schooldays, I thought, as my drinks were served.

'It's treasonable,' I said. 'I mean, if he's ever caught ...'

'We mustn't sit in judgement, chum. Ours not to reason why, and so on.'

As the cognac began to kick in, I wondered if this was really happening. 'He's the third most senior figure in the government.'

'Could be a trap, of course, a way of compromising your cousin, or even you. But I doubt it. My experience in life suggests that the most obvious explanations are invariably the true ones.'

He asked for his bill.

'It's the long game, chum. I just wonder if we'll be around to see the end of it.'

'Before you go, Vance.'

'Old boy?'

'That search I asked you to conduct.'

'As I mentioned before, I am making some progress. It happened a long time ago, but I would be cautiously optimistic.'

'Really?'

'Absolutely.'

'That would be wonderful.'

'Far too soon for celebrations,' he said, lighting a Gitanes.

Sugar was being escorted to the table by the head waiter, a man swathed in tails and wearing a celluloid collar.

'It's divine here,' she said. 'So pretty.'

'We must have a bet, for fun. You choose.'

She peered at me as she drank her Pimm's through a straw. 'Brandy, Marty? A bit early for you, I'd have thought.'

'We should bring the children here – when they're old enough,' I said.

'You're very paternal all of a sudden,' she said and looked to the next table, which stood empty under a pall of smoke.

9

DUBLIN

May 1969

I think of those as the good days, when we were still innocent, or largely so, when the basic structure of our lives was intact and had not yet been infected by all that would follow. I often think of Paris in the spring of 1969 as a line that we all crossed, in my case knowingly. I could, of course, blame Mr Haughey, for he was toxic, and no one who was associated with him, however marginally, escaped contamination – but back then I did not know that.

Bull Bridge was swallowed by sea mist and within moments Dublin was lost behind us.

'You look well. Paris obviously suited you,' she said and turned up the collar of her tan gabardine. 'Has there been any chatter since you returned? I mean, in your section?'

'About?'

'For example, has your Mr O'Neill made any reference to Mr Haughey that might make you suspect that Mr

O'Neill knows you met Mr Haughey in Paris? Or that O'Neill knows what Haughey is proposing to do?'

'Nothing.'

She nodded, as if I'd confirmed what she already believed to be the case. 'You see, we think he's genuine. Mr Haughey.'

'Genuine.'

'Confused, perhaps, but yes, genuine.'

'Not part of a trap then?'

Alison sighed. 'This is really very simple, Marty. Let's try to keep it that way, shall we?'

People kept looming from the mist, linked together, or pushing prams.

'Is Haughey working alone?' I asked.

'In a way. The man who's been running the show is Mr Blaney, your minister for agriculture from Donegal – we've had an asset embedded in his political apparatus for years. Mr Blaney is being briefed by radical republicans and passes this intelligence, or parts of it, on to Mr Haughey. Mr Haughey's approach to you is an attempt, one of several he is making, to establish his own contacts. He doesn't like or trust Mr Blaney and the feeling is entirely mutual. So if there is cash to arm the radicals, Mr Haughey wants to be the benefactor. He wants control. And also the glory. Mr Haughey considers himself to be a man of destiny. He sees you as one way in.'

'He's out of his mind. I have no contact with Iggy Kane or anyone else up there.'

'But Kane is your first cousin and so, when he receives Haughey's message via you, he'll know it's for real. Haughey knows this, which is why he picked you for the job.' Pearls of mist clung to the tips of Alison's dark brown hair. 'So please stop being pedantic.'

'Look, Iggy and I haven't met for years. I don't know him any more.'

'But you once knew him very well, I take it.'

'I know almost nothing of his life for the last seventeen years, except what I hear occasionally from people in Waterford. You probably know far more about him than I do.'

Alison nodded. 'His name does arise occasionally in the context of certain reports that have their origins in our intelligence services. They confirm that Kane is a minor player in a republican group in south Armagh.'

'Oh God, are you serious?'

'What was he like as a child?'

I thought for a moment. 'Very different.'

'There are many ways of being different.'

'Beyond the reach of any authority. He's severely dyslexic, which made some people think that he wasn't quite right in the head – but I never thought that. He was always a loner.'

Alison considered what I had said and then she sighed. 'Look, here's the position. He is indeed a minor player, in so far as he is not part of the new command structure that is evolving, but he is well regarded.'

'In what way?'

'We think Ignatius Kane is one of their electronics men.'

I wondered was this some kind of joke. 'Iggy? You means he's—'

'He's one of the names that keeps coming up in that connection, yes.'

'Christ, I don't believe it,' I said, even as I did.

'So Mr Haughey is astute to think that an approach to Kane coming through you will reach the right people in south Armagh, and that they, in turn, will convey that approach to the republican's new leadership.'

We could well have been out at sea together in a boat, lost in the elements.

'How does Haughey know the connection?'

'He has obviously done his homework.'

If I could have turned back then, I would have, but I felt borne along by something outside my control.

Alison said, 'However, it's better if you get in touch with Kane to relay Haughey's message through a third party. You'll know who to pick – one of those people who have kept in touch with him. After all, Marty, as a respected Irish diplomat you'll hardly want to be directly involved in something as sordid as giving cash to people whom we may soon be calling terrorists.'

She didn't even smile when she said this, just hiked up the collar of her coat. As we reached the end of the bridge and turned back, I thought of the other times she and I had met in recent years, and how much I had come to admire her. She knew my needs and had satisfied them without ever having to bring me to bed. At the same time, she had never withdrawn the ephemeral promise made in Waterloo, that she might be available to me in ways other than those concerned with intergovernmental business or military history. Now she was showing me a new side, as if everything that had previously passed between us was a mere preparation for the work at hand. My reaction surprised me, for I felt jilted in a strange and hopeless kind of way as I grasped that her interest in me was wider than affection.

'You look worried, Marty,' she said as we reached our cars. 'There's nothing to worry about. This is simply you conveying information. What?'

'This may all play into some grand design of yours,' I said, 'but if I am to do Haughey's bidding, I'll be helping republicans in Ulster and that's not something I'm very comfortable with.'

She almost smiled. 'Don't you think maybe you're exaggerating your own importance ever so slightly?'

'What do you mean?' I said, nettled despite myself.

'If you fail to pass on Mr Haughey's message to Kane, do you imagine Haughey will give up? Of course not. He's already put out feelers through other contacts. But if the contact is made through *you*, then at least we stay in.'

'If he gives them the cash, you know what they'll do with it, don't you?'

'Unfortunately, yes, but what choices do we have? Ireland is a sovereign country. We can't control what Mr Haughey does or what happens here. Occasionally we can make our presence felt, but otherwise we are detached observers.'

'Detached? I don't think so. You're major players and, as such, you should try and stop this from happening.'

This time she did smile. 'Come on, Marty. You know that only despots speak of trying to quash political movements that don't suit them. And even they don't always believe it can be done.'

'I'm trying to do what I think is best.'

'Indeed. And I for one have a very clear idea of what is best here. It is to get in early and stay in for the long haul. We're in the process of getting in.'

'But – for the long haul? This hasn't even begun yet.'

'With respect, your government hasn't the remotest idea what's going on in your own country. We, on the other hand, do. This way we stand the best chance of protecting our interests and, if I may say so, yours as well.'

She checked the time and took out her keys. 'Christopher and I so enjoyed Waterloo last time. I have never seen the children as happy and of course you know how much I adore it there. How is Sugar?'

I must have hesitated, for she missed nothing.

'Marty?'

'It's just—' I didn't want to tell her, since it seemed like a confidence too far, but then I realised that there was little this woman did not know. 'I'm not sure.'

'Go on.'

'This arrangement you and I have, my contact with Vance – it means I have to conceal things from Sugar and I hate doing that. I'm sure she senses it too – I can tell from the way she looks at me that she suspects something is going on. Maybe I was naïve, but this was not a problem I had anticipated.'

'Has she said anything?'

'She accuses me of being evasive, of concealing things. The problem is that I haven't yet mastered the art of dishonesty to the extent of being able to deceive the mother of my children.'

Alison winced. 'If it's any consolation, I understand. This is a lonely business, believe me. It's like a little club that no one else can join – not Christopher, not Sugar, not our children. But it's the price we pay for doing what we do. I, for one, believe that what I do is the right thing and so I'm prepared to pay that price. The question is, are you?'

'I don't know. I expect the answer is probably yes, but at times I really don't know.'

We stood there, damply, aware that we had become, in a way, partners, and that, barring something unforeseen, this was just the beginning of the road.

'You all right?'

'I think so.'

'Good, Marty, I knew you would be.' She bent forward to allow me to kiss her cheeks. 'You do know, don't you, that you're my favourite Irishman in the world.'

10

DUBLIN

July – August 1969

The North erupted. Riots became commonplace and our government really feared that the trouble could engulf the Republic. Mr Haughey's plans had succeeded alarmingly, even if I could not be sure that my contact with Iggy, which I had made through Bobby Gillece, had been the catalyst. On those occasions when Haughey came to Iveagh House for receptions, I made sure to keep well clear of him. And yet, in that beautiful summer, in our own jurisdiction, life was sweet.

'May I ask you something?' said Sugar.

It was a lovely evening in Rathgar, and the fragrance of sweet alyssum from the garden next door drifted in deliciously.

'Where exactly are your father's ashes?'

'My ... father's ashes?'

'I was putting flowers on your mother's grave in Waterford recently and I suddenly asked myself, where is your dad? Certainly not with your mother, or if he is, the headstone makes no mention of it. You see, if you and

I were hit by a bus next week, I would like to think we would be remembered together.'

'And so we shall be,' I said. 'Not that I've given much thought to it, but I know we can buy a grave in Ballyhale. Catholic, of course, because you Prods can't buy graves like we can, but if that's not a problem for you, Ballyhale it will be.'

Sugar tossed her head. 'It's not a problem at all for me, Marty, as long as we can be together.'

'Exactly. I'll see to it.' I poured white wine and sat back. 'I should visit my mother's grave more often. I really appreciate that you bring her flowers.'

Sugar took a deep breath and composed herself in the way her tennis opponents would have recognised. 'I loved your mother,' she said, with more than a hint of reprimand, 'even though I knew her only in her final years. We spoke a lot. She told me about your father – much more than you ever have.'

'Am I being criticised, or have I got that wrong?'

'You are annoyingly evasive, Marty.'

'I'm not sure I understand.'

'It means slippery, Marty. I ask you a question about your father's ashes and you slide out of giving me an answer. I wasn't brought up like that.'

'Where has all this come from? Here we are, having a quiet drink—'

'I've never tried to conceal anything from you – have I?'

'If you're referring to my father, I can't hold forth on someone who died when I was thirteen.'

'But you do remember him.'

'Of course.'

'You were at his funeral.'

'Is that a question or a statement of fact?'

'It's an assumption.'

'Well, you should be careful with your assumptions is my advice. I was sent home from school. My mother met me off the steamer and drove me to Waterloo where she insisted I have a gin and tonic. I learned then that my father had been dead for three weeks and had already been cremated. All that came home were his greatcoat, shoes, hat and wallet. We never discussed him after that. And since you raise your eyebrows, let me repeat what I have just said: we never discussed him again. And if you think what I've just described is strange, you don't understand the kind of house I grew up in. So, no, I did not attend his funeral, and no, I don't know where his ashes are.'

We sat without speaking for some moments.

'You're angry with me,' she said, 'but your reaction to my question is no surprise, just part of a pattern. Of you hiding things.'

'Such as?'

'Your work – what you do exactly. Now I get the impression that I'm not being told everything about your father.'

'Oh, I thought you said my mother had elaborated on him.'

'There's no point in being angry with her too.'

I made a point of gathering my thoughts. From where I sat, I could see seagulls form an arc on the Dublin skyline.

'Look, I'm sorry,' I said. 'You see, Nancy suited herself when it came to talking about my father. The fact is that I've searched high and low and I can't find him. The records of eight London crematoria have no record of him. My mother always refused to discuss it, even though

I pressed her. The Captain was insolvent, up to his neck with bookmakers and loan sharks. He could have disappeared and started a new life somewhere else. A new name. Fits him like a glove. He would only be in his early sixties. He could still be alive.'

'Oh, Marty.' Sugar's face radiated kindness. 'I'm sorry, I never realised.'

'It's like I'm forever living in a dream where one day he comes back.'

Sun warmed the back of my neck as I sat there, wondering why it had taken me so long to tell her, and then realised that I had been ashamed to do so.

'Your mother did talk to me about him. Towards the end,' Sugar said.

'What did she say?'.

'She told me that she adored him from the first moment they met. She was twenty and had never been in Dublin. He was on his way to England to fight the war. He asked her to marry him, there and then. She said he was ashamed of having grown up poor, but proud of the fact that his mother had given all of them a clean, ironed handkerchief every morning. He was ashamed they had no indoor plumbing and told her that his father had sat on a bucket in his bedroom after breakfast to empty his bowels and that it was Paddy's job to take out the slops. She told me that she loved him for everything – for his daring, his charm, his madness, his faults. He had seen terrible things during the war, she said, and the fact that he had kept his sense of humour, despite all that, made him her hero. She loved his style, and the dash they cut together at Epsom, or the Horse Show. He brought her to Covent Garden and they took a box. They stayed in

The Ritz and lunched at The Savoy where she once saw Winston Churchill at the next table. When Winston saw her, he smiled. None of that would have happened if she had stayed in Waterloo and never met Paddy, she said.'

I could see tears in my wife's eyes.

'Look, I regret not having spent more time with her,' I said, 'particularly towards the end.'

'It was woman's talk.'

'I'm sorry if I have upset you.'

'I just wished I had had a mother like that.' Sugar sniffed. 'I was pregnant during her last months. She used to laugh at me and say that she hoped for my sake that my baby wasn't as big as you had been. I asked her had it been very painful. She said it could have been worse. "When you ride horses as a girl it spreads your hips and everything between them. I just popped him out," she said.'

Did the past ever take place? I wondered. Did it ever tangibly occur? Or had I imagined it?

'What else did she tell you?'

'Oh, this and that.'

'Such as?'

'She had lung cancer, Marty; she was on a lot of medication. Sometimes she didn't make sense.'

'Nonetheless...'

Sugar bit her lip. 'She once said something quite odd.'

'Really?'

'We were chatting about, I don't know, where I would send Emmet to school, something like that, or at least I was doing most of the talking, because she used to get quite drowsy, and then, completely out of the blue, she said, "Fred Black was Paddy's ruination."'

'She said that?'

'Yes, she did. I asked her who Fred Black was, but she'd gone to sleep. I tried again the next day, but she just looked at me.'

'Fred Black,' I said.

'That was the name she said, yes. Who was he?'

I felt a weight on my chest. 'I don't know,' I said as our neighbour started up his lawnmower. 'Any more than I know where my father's ashes are. I simply don't know.'

11

DUBLIN
SHELBOURNE HOTEL

Late December 1951

A young, fair-haired maid was unpacking my mother's clothes and carefully placing them in drawers that smelled of mothballs. She reminded me of a time I could not quite remember, but which was warm and intensely pleasant, and I wanted to drink in her pleasingly round figure and her anxious but pretty face from which her fair hair had been tied back beneath a white cap, and, from where I lay on my parents' bed, I could see that above one of her knees her stocking was laddered. After Waterloo, which my parents had barely had time to open up before leaving it again, the Shelbourne was blissfully warm. Nonetheless I felt sad. Iggy and his dad had been due to leave Waterford that day for good. By now they would have reached their new home on the border.

'I'm going to the bar to meet that man.' The Captain upended his gin, slapped his cheeks with Old Spice, combed back the greying wings of his hair and stood upright. 'Everyone on best behaviour, aye?'

'For God's sake!' Nancy said, lighting a cigarette. 'You lie down with dogs, you get up with fleas.'

I found it curious how my father's various smells lingered after him – the sharp hit of his aftershave lotion, the faint sweat that always clung to his jackets, his boot polish.

'Oh God! Marty?' My mother sounded husky, as she did every evening at this time. 'Marty? Come here, pet, and clip me!' She sat hopelessly at the dressing table, a string of pearls in her hands, the cigarette in her mouth.

'I can't seem to close it.'

I knew these pearls, which were taken out for special occasions; the catch was worn and hard to fasten to the tiny eyelet, which I now attempted to do.

'I hate these evenings,' she said. 'A lot of fuss for nothing.'

As I laid my hands on her neck with its little race of golden hairs, and thought about the maid who had just left, and was wondering if my mother would mind if I bent down and kissed her neck, she leant forward for her lipstick.

'Don't move, Mummy.'

Her smoky-green eyes sought me out from the mirror.

'Well done,' she said, testing the necklace, getting up, draining her glass, pouting at her image in the dress with the huge collar, reaching for her fox stole and evening bag. 'Well done, love.'

Holly boughs adorned the lift. She took my arm and, when I looked at her in surprise, smiled beautifully. From the hall, I could hear the Captain's whinnying laugh. In the Horseshoe Bar, a small, dapper individual with a goatee beard stood beside my father.

'Ah-ha!' cried the Captain. 'Better late than never!'

My mother allowed the goateed man to kiss her cheeks.

'Champagne, my dear?' he enquired in what I would later learn was a Cockney accent.

'Do fish swim?' shouted the Captain and the other man harrumphed.

'Thank you, Fred,' my mother said. 'This is Martin, our son. This is Mr and Mrs Black, Marty.'

Next to Mr Black, a fat woman with hooped, gypsy-like earrings and wearing a low-cut dress that was bright as silver-plate, sat on a barstool. Beside her, on another stool, sat a girl about my age, her bare legs crossed.

'Pleased to meet you, Martin, I'm sure,' said Mrs Black. 'You're a fine big lad, aren't you?'

'I've worked it out that by the time he's seventeen, he's going to have cost me eleven grand,' the Captain said. 'Eleven grand!'

'Good thing you're loaded then, Paddy,' said Mr Black and winked at me. 'Martin, meet my daughter, Daisy.'

'Hello,' I said.

She brushed back her fair hair and slid her glance sideways, as if inviting me to look for something whose location was known to her alone.

'Daisy's not been herself after the crossing,' her mother said.

'I'll need more than a few winners to pay for this chap's education, let me tell you!' barked the Captain, in full performance mode. 'I'm taking him with me to London next year. Show him the sights, you know? We'll stay in my club on Piccadilly.'

'Oh, really?' said Mr Black.

'The In and Out Club,' my father said. 'I often buy Anthony Eden a drink there. Anthony Eden.'

'He's a smashing looking bloke, Anthony Eden,' said Mrs Black. 'I love his hats.'

'Asked me to call him Tony,' said the Captain, his expression wild. 'The new Foreign Secretary! D'you know what he told me? That Churchill sleeps all day, pissed as a newt! Anthony Eden told me that, in the members' bar, true as you're standing there! Churchill!'

'Now, Martin, let me tell you something,' said Mr Black, drawing me to one side. 'You listen to your dad, you hear me? He and I are very good friends. Your dad's a very clever man.'

A diamond tiepin burned just above the buttons of his waistcoat. I could see Nancy blowing smoke from the side of her mouth, her way of telling me that she loathed these people.

'The trouble is what to do with cash,' I heard Mr Black tell my father as a man dressed like a spiv suddenly appeared at Mr Black's elbow.

'Mmm,' said Mr Black, listening. 'Just wait a sec.' He turned to the Captain. 'Ollie here keeps his ear to the ground – don't you, Ollie?'

'As close to it as I can, boss.'

'A Basset Hound, if ever there was one, our Ollie. And what do you hear, Ollie? You can tell the Captain.'

Ollie leaned in and the lights from the bar sparked off his hair gel. 'I hear thirteen-to-two trap one, Harold's Cross last race this evening,' he hissed.

'Mmm,' said Mr Black again. He nodded once to Ollie. 'The usual.'

'Consider it done, boss.'

As Ollie made to leave, Mr Black called out. 'One sec, Ollie. Paddy? D'you want on?'

Consternation flooded my father's face. He slapped the pockets of his jacket and smiled crookedly.

'Don't really follow the dogs,' he said.

'Nonsense. I insist,' said Mr Black. He flashed out a pair of tenners. 'Have a hundred and thirty to a score on for the Captain as well, and be quick about it!'

'Consider it done,' said Ollie again.

'Happy, Paddy?'

The Captain's face was lit by a foolish grin. 'Well, yes, thank you very much, Fred.'

The menus had arrived in the hands of a head waiter dressed in a black tailcoat.

'We had the beef here last night. I just love it, don't you?' said Mrs Black to Nancy.

'I love the fish in the Russell,' my mother said.

'Ever thought of putting a few dogs into training?' Mr Black asked my father. 'Beef done rare.'

'Certainly, Mr Black.'

'I know just the man to start you off,' Mr Black said.

'Your table is ready now, Mr Black.'

'A hundred and thirty to a score,' the Captain whispered, and I saw Nancy roll her eyes as we made our way across the hall to the dining room.

Never before had I seen the Captain in a group of which he was not the obvious leader and, of course, he had just now as good as accepted money, something he had always forbidden me to do. In the restaurant, Mr Black sat at the head of the table and ordered the wine. Occasionally, he whispered to my father, whereupon the Captain sat back, blinking for a moment, then let out a whistle of air.

Mr and Mrs Black ordered asparagus; my father did

the same. I'd never heard of asparagus. When the rectangular dishes arrived, the Captain took a knife and fork to his, and cut the asparagus into little pieces, but the Blacks used their fingers to pick up the green spears and dip them in melted butter. A pianist raced up and down his keyboard, turning to the room for applause after each melody was concluded. The Captain had become ever more expansive, referring to upcoming business deals that even I knew were unlikely to arise.

'Quite nice the suites here, aren't they?' Mrs Black observed as our main course was served.

'Poor Marty has to sleep on the sofa in ours,' my mother said.

'Oh, really? Do you not have a second bedroom?' asked Mrs Black. 'Ours has a second bedroom.'

'*What?*'

'It doesn't matter, Paddy, we're perfectly fine as we are,' Nancy said.

'Did you say your suite has two bedrooms?' I could tell by my father's glinting stare that he had picked up the scent of an enemy.

'It's what we're normally given in a decent hotel,' said Mrs Black.

'Two bedrooms?' my father said.

'Well, we're only staying here because you recommended it,' said Mrs Black.

'Very nice, too, Paddy, well done you,' said Mr Black.

'D'you know how long *I've* been coming here?' the Captain said grimly. 'Nineteen bloody forty.'

'That long really?' said Mr Black.

'And they fob me off with a shitty little one-bedroom suite.'

'People have no respect any more, have they?' said Mr Black sadly. 'The times we live in.'

'I'll show them a thing or two about respect,' said the Captain and threw down his napkin.

'Oh, God!' cried Nancy. 'Leave it alone, Paddy.'

'Bloody Bolsheviks!'

'The fact is,' said Mr Black, 'when you're generous to them, all they do is come along and take advantage of you.'

'I expect because it's our first time they were trying to make a good impression,' Mrs Black said.

'I'll make an impression on somebody,' the Captain snarled, pushing back his chair. '*Waiter!*'

I was conscious of sudden silence. A stooped, bald little man in a white jacket appeared.

'Yes, sir?'

'Get me the manager.'

'Yes, sir.'

As Mr Black looked across to his wife, and their eyes met, I realised all at once that my father was no match for these people, which made me hate them.

'Yes, Captain?' The head waiter was beside my father's chair.

'Are you the manager?'

'Not yet, Captain, unfortunately,' said the head waiter in a brave attempt at joviality, 'but what can I do for you?'

'I asked for the manager,' the Captain said. 'Get him.'

'If anything's the matter with dinner, Captain, you should tell me.'

'The dinner is perfectly adequate,' said my father. 'The problem is with the attitude of the people who run this *fucking hotel!*'

I could see Mr Black absorbing the unfolding situation with a little smile. The piano had gone quiet. Everyone in the dining room was looking at my father, except for Daisy. She was looking at me, and when I smiled, the point of her tongue emerged like the head of a hungry worm and tapped the lovely little indentation at the centre of her upper lip.

'Captain,' the head waiter said with a deep breath, 'it's ten o'clock. The manager is off-duty, and I must ask you to show some respect to the other diners.'

'Was I shown respect?' the Captain cried. 'Was it respectful to put me and my family into a cubbyhole?'

My mother stood up. 'I'm going to bed. Good night, and thank you very much for dinner, Fred.'

'*You will sit down!*' roared the Captain, like someone beyond the reach of land.

'Captain . . .' the waiter began.

My father was on his feet. 'D'you know what I'm going to do? I'm going to buy this hotel and sack the Bolsheviks who run it. Then we'll see who shows me and my family the respect we deserve.'

Black was helping Nancy arrange her stole as the pianist struck up a lively number and the formerly curious customers at other tables were shaking their heads.

'Have I been unreasonable?' the Captain asked Mr Black. 'Have I stepped out of line?'

'Not one inch, Paddy,' said Mr Black, 'not one inch.'

'You,' the Captain said to the head waiter, 'get your black tail out to the telephone and tell the manager that I don't care what time it is, Captain Ransom wants to see him in here, now! D' you understand? *Now!*'

Daisy smiled at me as her tongue swam out again and

beckoned me with a little movement of its curled wet tip. All at once, the intense physical need I had felt when Auntie Kate had washed my hair in Fowler Street swept through me.

'Captain, I'll have to ask you to leave,' the waiter said, taking my father's elbow.

'Get your fucking hands off me!'

'Please, sir …'

'Allo, allo.' Mr Black was looking towards the door.

It took me a few seconds to recognise Ollie from earlier in the evening.

'Good night to you, Ollie,' said Mr Black. 'How has your evening been?'

A smile split Ollie's narrow face and he stuck both thumbs in the air. 'Winner all right!' he chortled. 'Winner all right!'

Nancy kept saying she wished we could go home. Although I never wanted to meet Mr Black again, I had spent the night on my made-up bed dreaming of Daisy.

'It's our turn to entertain the Blacks tonight,' the Captain said and honked the horn as we overtook a double-decker bus. 'I've booked a table in Jammet's.'

'How much is that going to cost, Paddy?'

'Who cares?' my father cried. 'It's the bookmakers who'll be paying!'

'We should have used the money you won to pay our bill in the hotel,' she said.

'Fuck that hotel.'

As if everything was being synchronised by forces unknown, the Blacks' maroon Bentley, driven by a uniformed chauffeur, glided by and I could see Daisy staring out, her pale face empty of interest.

'I don't trust him, Paddy,' said my mother. 'He's just appeared from nowhere, like a toadstool.'

'Have you ever found a hundred and thirty quid under a toadstool?' snapped the Captain.

'We can't afford to mix with these kinds of people any more,' Nancy said. 'He's a professional gambler.'

'I know exactly what he is,' the Captain said. 'He trusts me to have money on for him. You saw what happened last night? This is the opportunity of a lifetime.'

'I have a bad feeling,' Nancy said.

As soon as we had parked and walked up the hill to Leopardstown, my father hurried off, like someone already late for an appointment. Nancy and I found the damp tearooms, where she ordered tea and an elaborate stand of cakes, but then discovered, when we had finished, that she had no money to pay for it.

'My husband will pay,' she told the manager as we paraded out and she went to the ladies' room.

I huddled at the end of a building, watching horses being led around and the owners waiting for their jockeys. All at once I saw Daisy, tall, elegant and beautiful to my eyes, standing with her parents. An official in a white coat stuck his arm out.

'Owners and trainers, sonny,' he said. 'Get lost.'

Staring in, aching to be near her, I was overwhelmed by the sense that she and I were on the one side of something I had only just discovered. I did not know then that I would never see her again, or that the image of her lovely face would stay with me for many years.

When the Captain reappeared, he was perspiring.

'Are you involved here?' Nancy asked.

'Number six belongs to Fred,' said the Captain from clenched teeth.

All I remember after that is my father's ashen face, and our swift departure from the racecourse, during which I did not dare remind them of the unpaid tearoom bill, and our surprising drive directly back to Waterloo, a three-hour journey, without bothering to collect our luggage from the Shelbourne. Little was said and the smoke from my parents' cigarettes filled the car. Although Waterloo was wrapped in night, Danny was standing outside the front door, with Eileen beside him, wiping her tears. I wondered how she knew that my father had backed a loser.

'What now?' the Captain barked, jumping out.

I heard low talk and knew they didn't want me to hear.

'Oh, Jesus,' Nancy said.

'Some children found him,' I heard Eileen say.

'How found him?' my father snapped.

'In the old forge in Jail Street,' Danny said. 'An anvil fell on him. Killed him straightaway.'

My mother began to wail.

'Christ, shut up!' the Captain cried. 'God forgive me but he's better off.'

'He was your brother, Paddy, even if he was retarded,' Nancy sniffled.

'What a bloody mess,' the Captain said.

12

DUBLIN

June 1971

We had moved to a more spacious house, in Sandymount, just five minutes from the beach to which Nurse Fleming brought Emmet, and Georgie, our daughter, every day. Sugar played tennis competitively in Fitzwilliam. On most weekends, we drove down to Waterloo, where Alison and Christopher were frequent visitors. On the last occasion they had stayed, a plan to go on holiday to Malta had been discussed. In Iveagh House, I was part of an ever-expanding team whose goal was to finally make Ireland a member of the European Economic Community. My work was valued, particularly when small concessions were needed from my counterparts on the British side.

Charles Haughey had been arrested on charges of conspiring to import arms and had left office in disgrace. It was an international sensation. Even though Haughey was subsequently acquitted, it would be five years before he was allowed back into government. My meeting with him in Paris seemed to have been forgotten, for which I was grateful, since I had feared that he might refer to it during his trial, but he never had.

Domestic economic issues were beginning to dominate the political debate. I continued to brief Alison on matters that would interest her, including those files on Ulster that Bill O'Neill sometimes left lying on his desk, or information stamped for Bill's attention from the nearby Department of Justice.

Sugar had become impatient with me over small things, such as jobs around the farm left undone, or promises to the children unfulfilled, charges I always defended by pleading commitments at work. It had long been accepted that during the week in Dublin my homecoming was unpredictable, to the extent that our having dinner together had become an exception. I put Sugar's darker humour down to the toil of the many tensions I held within myself and must have been projecting.

One Friday, as we drove into the south-east, when I asked casually what time Alison and Christopher were expected – for they had been invited for the weekend – Sugar, at the wheel, said, 'They're not coming.'

'Oh, really? Why not?'

'Because I rang them up and cancelled them.'

'*Cancelled* them?'

'Yes, Marty. Do you have a problem with that?'

Nurse Fleming and the children had become unusually still. We drove for another hour in silence, until our mountain appeared.

'Will you bring me fishing, Daddy, please?' asked Emmet.

'Perhaps. Let's get unpacked first and we'll see.'

'Daddy's far too busy to go fishing,' Sugar said and drove the car down the hill and over the lake bridge in a shower of pebbles.

Later, when the children had gone out with tadpole nets, we stood in the kitchen, the deal table between us.

'Why did you cancel the Chases without telling me?'

'Is she that bloody important to you, Marty? That we can't come down here for a weekend without her lumbering after us? With her supercilious know-it-all expression on her big face? You love it, don't you, all that English shit about history and shires and the war? Well, I'm sick to the back teeth of it.'

She was not to be diverted.

'I just don't know you any more. I haven't a clue what's going on inside you, or where that thing, whatever it is, is taking you. It's as if I'm being continually deceived.'

'I'm not deceiving you.'

'Are you screwing her? It would be easier if you told me the truth.'

Yes, it would have been simpler had I been conducting a traditional affair, rutting in cars and in the rooms of cheap hotels.

'I have never loved anyone but you since the day we married. Nor do my plans involve departing from that standard.'

'Then what is it that makes you the way you are? You're like a man who's been hollowed out. What is it?'

I cursed myself for putting all I loved in jeopardy for the sake of something I scarcely understood. 'My position is complicated. Occasionally I have to inhabit a sort of no-man's-land in order to discharge my duties. It isn't easy.'

'I didn't marry a civil servant, Marty. I married a farmer with a romantic home in the hills. Now you clock in and out, you never tell me anything. We never talk anymore – do you realise that? And yet when Alison bloody Chase is around, you never shut up – whispering to her when you think other people aren't looking, staying up together long after everyone else has gone to bed. It's nauseating.'

I felt as if my foundations, never altogether reliable, were about to crumble.

'Sugar, I'm not an accountant or a vet. What I mean is, I don't have a job that lends itself to discussion at home. Alison and I – well, our work occasionally overlaps, as you can imagine. And yes, there are certain subjects that cannot be discussed formally, at intergovernmental level. So I suppose we do tend to swap policies now and then, when we meet socially, on a one-to-one basis, which I accept is inconsiderate and ill-mannered, and for which I apologise. It won't happen again.'

'What subjects?'

'Sorry?'

'What are the subjects that cannot be discussed formally at intergovernmental level? What exactly are the ideas you swap with her when you and she are down by the lake, pretending to be interested in the children fishing? What do you drone on about long after Christopher has passed out and I've gone to bed?'

'Well, I can't exactly say.'

'Oh? Because you've forgotten? Or because you can tell her things that you can't tell me?'

'It's not like that, Sugar. Alison and I—'

'Well then what is it like, Marty? What does she know that I don't?'

'There are such things as secrets,' I said, knowing how pompous and pathetic that sounded. 'Official secrets.'

She stared at me. 'Are you telling me you're some sort of spy?'

It took all my resources to maintain my composure, for what she had just said – the word she had used – hit me in the gut like a mallet.

'Of course I'm not,' I said, trying not to bluster. 'I'm just an executive officer in a government department.'

She stared. 'My God, look at you! You've gone pale!'

'Sugar...'

'I think you are! You're a spy! You're giving her information, aren't you? Stuff you can't give her officially. Does she pay you for that? If she does, I'm damned if I know where the money goes.'

'Sugar, please.'

'Deny it then. Go on.'

'Of course she's not paying me. There's nothing to pay me for.'

'Let's face it, Marty, she wouldn't have to pay you, would she? You'd much prefer to be working for Alison and her lot in Whitehall than for Bill O'Neill – admit it!'

'Sugar, I'm not a spy!' I shouted, more in terror than anger. 'Stop this!'

'Or maybe she's the spy, feeding you information! Which makes you both spies. Oh, Christ, what have we got into? God help me and my children.' She sat down heavily, her gaze on something distant that did not include me. 'You're impossible to engage with,' she said with a resignation that made me despise myself.

'I'm doing my best to describe my job.'

'I hate it, I hate it, I hate it.' She pressed her hands to

her temples. 'I've always supported you, changed my life in order to marry you and lived like a shrew ever since. I've carried more than my share of the work and the worry. We've drifted apart. Why? You tell me there's not another woman, and I believe you. So it has to be this work of yours. If your work is above board and decent, then say so. But if you're doing something wrong, then you should stop.'

'I'm doing nothing wrong,' I said, trying my utmost to believe it, wishing that Alison were there, for she could have explained better than me what I was doing, and why.

'I hate your job, Marty, which is most unhealthy, because it's leading me to hate you. I live in the shadow of what you do. I sit some days and cry for the whole morning, not knowing why I'm crying, and then realise it's because much of the time I'm married to a stranger.'

I felt cut because I knew she was at least partly right.

'I'm just lucky I have Fleming. She's so kind and helpful.'

'You ... discuss this with Fleming?'

'She knows. Women know. She supports me, and I'm very grateful to her.'

Sugar was suddenly calm, in an almost eerie way. 'I actually decided to leave you, Marty. My parents know how I feel. There's room for the children and me in Carlow, although Fleming will have to leave. I had made my mind up.'

'"Had"?'

She shook violently. 'My father has cancer.'

I could not speak.

'It's inoperable. He has only a few months to live. I'm

not landing in on my parents in the circumstances. Unfortunately, I have to stay here with you.'

'Sugar, I'm so sorry.'

'Don't, please,' she said as I reached for her.

'I'll leave,' I said.

'Where would you go? To a digs in Leeson Street so you can be near your office? Be near her?'

'I mean I'll leave the job. Not immediately, but at the end of the year. I'll have certain entitlements by then.'

She looked at me sadly. 'You'll never leave it. It owns you.'

'I never saw it as anything more than a means to keep us going, to pay for Waterloo.'

'I'll believe it when I see it.'

'I'm a free man! I'll do what I want, and if leaving my job means saving my marriage, that's what I'll do.'

And then I was on my knees, holding her around the waist, her warm belly to my face as the poverty of my life overwhelmed me.

13

DUBLIN

1972

The New Year began badly. On the penultimate day of January, a Sunday, thirteen male civilians were shot dead in Derry by the British Army. We were in Waterloo when the telephone rang, an unusual event, since I had given few people the number. It was Alison.

'Christ!' I said when she told me. 'This is disgraceful.'

'We're on it,' she said. 'This evening we're announcing a sworn inquiry, chaired by a very senior judge. If there was wrongdoing it will be exposed quickly and efficiently. We are urging everyone to be calm.'

'More than your fucking Tommies were,' I said.

We drove back to Dublin, listening to the non-stop coverage. That evening I went into Iveagh House where there was pandemonium as the extent of the massacre became clear. The world's media was flocking to Derry. It was the only time I saw Bill O'Neill ruffled. He was wearing a shaggy tweed jacket over a thick, green polo neck, and his hair was wild, as if he had come directly from a cliff top or a windy beach.

'This is a disaster,' he kept saying. 'This could tip the scales.'

'It's an outrage,' I said. 'We may as well still be a colony as far as the Brits are concerned.'

'The Brits!' Bill's face had drained and the knuckles of the hand that held his pipe stood out. 'You know something? If I was a young man again I'd be up there in south Armagh with those lads, helping them blow fucking British soldiers to smithereens!' His eyes blazed as his anger briefly got the upper hand; then he suddenly realised what he had said and to whom he had said it.

'I didn't mean that, Marty. I apologise.'

'Forget it; it's fine.'

'It's not fine. I'm a senior diplomat and you're not just a trusted colleague, you're ex-British Army, so I was way out of order there.'

'Look, Bill, I understand. I feel exactly the same way. What happened is unforgivable.'

A telephone rang and he picked it up. 'The minister again,' he said as he replaced the receiver and grimaced, as if he was allergic to politicians. 'Marty, just in case you think—'

'Say no more, Bill. It's been a dreadful day, and we're all very upset.'

'I appreciate your understanding.'

'It never happened. We never had this discussion.'

'That's very decent of you, Marty.'

'You'd better not keep the minister waiting,' I said.

The bloodbath seemed to go to the core of every Irishman and woman, even Irishmen like me with dreams of empire. My father would have felt the same, I was sure, for this was more than an abuse of friendship. This was war.

And yet the work of government continued, and so did I, in my job, despite my promises to Sugar. Our minister, inclined to regard himself as a figure on the international stage, needed to be restrained from making telephone calls to the press. The Taoiseach went on television looking like a man who had just received a terminal diagnosis. Never in recent years had we been further from the Brits.

'We are appalled,' Alison said two days later as we sat in her car on Dollymount Strand. 'The military have circled the wagons, but there's little doubt they ran amok.'

'There's a sense of outrage I've never seen before.'

'Tell me about it. Yesterday we were under siege for three hours. Rocks, ball-bearings, you name it, bouncing off the embassy's windows. It's a wonder we weren't ransacked.'

The department had called in her ambassador, and reprimanded the British Army in stark language, even as we endeavoured to defuse the situation at unofficial level.

'We can't apologise, of course, without appearing to betray the army,' Alison said. 'But we are sorry, believe me.'

'Sorry you've been caught on the hop, more likely. Excuse my language, but your people are shits of the highest order. You have undercover agents, probably SAS, roaming Belfast, collecting information and taking pot shots at Provo suspects. You're up to your necks with the Loyalists, colluding in their dirty work, sponsoring them, like you sponsored the IRA a few years ago.'

For once, Alison was quiet. 'I told you, Marty. We are sorry.'

'Actions speak louder than words.'

'Look,' she said, 'I've been told that we'll be pushing as hard as we can to support your application for EEC membership.'

'You're such hypocrites. It's obvious that if you're let in, we must be let in, too. You would much prefer not to have a land border with a non-EEC country.'

'We won't go so far as to say that if you don't get in we won't go in, but we'll go bloody close,' Alison said. 'Give us some credit.'

'We need some heads on sticks, Alison.'

'Lord Widgery is the most respected judge in England. You'll get your heads on sticks, but it will take time.' She looked at her watch. 'I've got to get back. Ask your people to try and call the hounds off, would you?'

Palm trees bowed to the wind, adding to the sense of apocalypse.

'Next Thursday, they're burying their dead in Derry,' I said. 'Down here we're declaring a day of public mourning. There will be another demonstration in Dublin.'

'We've already officially requested your army to protect our embassy.'

'The request will be denied,' I said. 'I suggest you call in sick that day.'

She took my advice. Four days later, the British Embassy was set alight by a mob, and in early March the Provisional IRA bombed the Abercorn Restaurant in central Belfast, killing two young women and wounding more than a hundred and thirty people, many of whom would never walk or see again. Despite the tension that screamed from every front page and editorial, the Brits stuck to their word and the door to Europe was suddenly open to Ireland. On 10th May, when our EEC referendum took place, and was carried by an overwhelming margin, a spontaneous party took place in Iveagh House, during which my section was singled out for praise.

14

DUBLIN

1974

They say that all war is spent in a kind of helpless suspension, waiting, waiting, for the final battle, the final death, the final capitulation. Waiting for the great collective sigh of human relief that rises to heaven when the whole wretched business eventually concludes and the dead are left in peace. That was how it felt during those early years of the nineteen seventies in Ireland, for, even though we in the Republic were not at war, less than two hours' drive away young men and women were killing one another, and their neighbours, in a spiral of violence that no one knew how to mitigate or end. It was as if the bad government that Vance had described to me had led to an orgy of death that was ravening not just Northern Ireland but spilling down over the border and across the Irish Sea.

In the first week of February, nine British soldiers and three civilians were blown to pieces by a Provo bomb on a coach travelling on the M62 in Yorkshire. The daily news was terrifying and in March that terror came south, to Dublin and Monaghan. Thirty-three civilians were killed and more than three hundred injured by Loyalist bombs. The Provos retaliated. In June, they bombed the Houses of Parliament in London, injuring eleven people and causing enormous damage.

We walked in the shadows of trees as deer moved ahead of us through the Phoenix Park undergrowth. It was September and an Indian summer had taken hold.

'It's been some time.'

'It's the way this thing goes,' she said.

Since we no longer socialised with the Chases, these meetings were now confined to cups of coffee in suburban cafés, drinks in pubs, or strolls, such as this, in open spaces.

'I thought you had forgotten me,' I said, knowing how peeved that sounded.

'Oh, come on! It's been a matter of waiting for the right moment.'

She'd been out in the sun and her face had an attractive eddy of freckles across the nose. Scents of wild honeysuckle and dog roses lay on the still air as bats darted for the insect hatches.

'I sometimes wonder if this is all a ridiculous game,' I said, 'not just the work we do together occasionally, but, you know, the whole, tortuous political waterwheel we spend our lives on. Look at history, look at the decisions that led to both world wars, made by men who were arrogant or crazy or stupid, or all three. It's no different now, whatever we may think. People will keep on dying violently for their warped political beliefs, no matter what you and I try to do about it.'

'And yet the moment we cease to try, we rob our lives

of meaning,' she said. 'We have to keep trying to do the right thing.'

'Whatever that is.'

She smiled, a little sadly, and chose the bole of a tree to lean against. 'I had hoped for a practical as opposed to a philosophical discussion, Marty.'

'Meaning?'

'That the time has arrived for you to make an even more important contribution than you have been doing. Now especially.'

'Events,' I said.

'Atrocities, I would say. And you know of at least one person who is behind them.'

Her voice was flat and cold.

'Just a minute,' I said. 'Who are you talking about?'

'There are three experienced bomb manufacturers in south Armagh and he is one of them.'

Pain entered my chest. 'You don't mean Iggy Kane?'

'Unfortunately, I do.'

I could see the determination in her face. 'How can you be sure?' I asked.

'You mean, apart from having had intelligence on him for more than five years?'

'He could have retired,' I said, resisting her reprimand. 'He could have reformed.'

Her expression was that of someone indulging a stubborn but much-loved child. 'One of Ignatius Kane's half-brothers, with whom he lives, sold a car last month. We found traces of nitro-glycerine in it,' she said.

'Inconclusive.'

'And flecks of paint that correspond to the Yorkshire bomb.'

'But not in Iggy's car,' I said as I simultaneously wondered if this was really happening.

She sighed as if she finally had more important matters to deal with than my irritating observations. 'I'm sorry, but he's a monster, Marty. I've seen the pictures – afterwards. Of the victims. *His* victims.'

Was the coal fire in Fowler Street an illusion too, I wondered? Which part of the world in which I lived was real, which fake?

'Look,' I said, 'I don't care about myself, but please don't involve my family.'

She shook her head vigorously. 'He knows exactly what he's doing. He knows exactly where the bombs are going and who's going to die. He knows exactly what happens when you pack ball-bearings into a steel canister with explosives and ignite them on a bus by means of a radio signal. He knows exactly what the devastation will be to the men, women and children on that bus. A monster.'

'Then you created the monster.'

'Oh, for goodness sake!' She tossed her head impatiently. 'Grow up, Marty!'

'Why pick him? Why not pick on one of the other bomb-makers? You said that there are three.'

She smiled faintly, as if my naïvety was endearing. 'Because we don't have a direct line to the other bomb-makers, do we?'

My breath was short and I wondered if I was going mad.

'Years ago, after Paris, I told you this would happen, but you didn't want to hear,' I said.

'I don't make strategy, I'm just employed. Governments come and go. We don't try to solve problems, we try to contain them, and when we fail, as we currently are, we try something else. The best we can hope for in Northern Ireland is to hold the field. We accept that. But every so often we have to make our presence felt.'

In the near distance, cars with sidelights streamed through the park.

'Which is why we're going to remove him.'

I went deaf. 'Remove him?'

'Yes, absolutely.'

'You can't do that. He's got a wife. People depend on him.'

'Marty.' Alison was at her most uncompromising. 'Please listen. Ignatius Kane is a particularly abhorrent little shit, and yes, if we'd known after Paris just how dangerous he is we probably would not have approved of your using him as a route for Mr Haughey's largesse. But we did and you did, and now Mr Haughey has been banished and here we all are. This is a war, although nobody admits it, and Ignatius Kane knows exactly what to expect in a war. He is now a high priority for us. You are our very dear friend, for whom we have the utmost regard. I know that you must recoil in horror, as we do, when you see the results of his actions. We need you in this now, Marty.'

As her brown eyes shone from her pretty face, I wanted to hold her close and breathe in her strength and conviction.

'I can't do it,' I said. 'We grew up together. Forget it.'

'And allow him to continue murdering innocent people? You don't want that and neither do I.'

'Of course not. But what you're asking is impossible.'

'I haven't asked anything of you yet. I was merely

taking the opportunity to tell you that we intend to stop a psychopath in his tracks, in the hope that you would support us.'

I think I had long wondered when this moment would come and, when it did, how it would be put. In the dimness of the trees, I started up a cigarette. 'How?' I asked.

'Leave that to us.'

'I cannot and will not be involved in anything you are planning in the Republic, however indirectly.'

'We don't operate in the Republic, Marty,' she said with more than a hint of condescension. 'And neither does he, for that matter.'

'And I don't operate, as you put it, in the Six Counties.'

Alison heaved another sigh. 'This will take place within our own jurisdiction, quite lawfully. Not that it will stop the bombs, of course, but it will send a message. Are you on side?'

'Let me think about it. Do I have a choice?'

'You've always had a choice, and, if I may say so, you've always chosen well.' Her hand was on my arm. 'Whatever we decide, no one will ever suspect your part, and that's paramount. This will take time, but I'll let you know.'

'I'm not saying—' I began.

'Say nothing,' she said. 'Reflect on the situation.'

'But—'

She laid a finger on my lips. Deer had crept out and were so near I could see the breath from their muzzles.

'Try to keep this separate from your private life, will you? I know it's not easy – look at me. I call it the tyranny of secrets. Christopher and I haven't had a relationship for years – sometimes I wonder if we were ever in love.

You and Sugar, on the other hand, have something very precious, and I would hate to see that damaged.'

I sighed. 'All this has very nearly ruined my marriage.'

'I am sorry.'

'I think she knows what's going on. She once asked me if I was a spy.'

'I know, Marty. I know.'

I peered at her. 'How do you know?'

'She told Christopher,' Alison said, 'and Christopher told me.'

15

On a cloudless Saturday evening I watched a hurling match from the sideline with Bobby Gillece. Three stones overweight, his ginger moustache patchy with the years, Bobby struggled to catch his breath. Bobby and Kate had no children. Sometimes, in Bobby's Bar, when she and I came face to face, and I remembered, albeit for an instant, how much she had once meant to me, she had just smiled politely, as she might to any customer.

Since my Phoenix Park meeting with Alison, I had lived in almost perpetual dread of her next phone call, for I knew what it would mean. I was often dizzy, trying to come to terms with my position, the situation I now found myself in. As I attempted to find my courage I had come back to my roots.

'Ted and I used to play matches out here,' Bobby said, 'when we were twelve or thirteen years old. Or Ted used to play and I used to try and not get in the way. God, he was good. I can see him this minute, out there, climbing into the air for the *sliothair*, higher than anyone else.

Even then, he was head and shoulders above the rest of us.'

Ash echoed as four players went for the same falling ball.

'We used to get our hurleys from a man up on the Yellow Road,' Bobby said. 'He had a little factory set up in a shed behind the house. I can still remember the smell of the wood shavings and the sawdust. He'd take one look at you to measure you, and then if he didn't have the right hurley for you, he'd make one, there and then. Ted liked a stick with an extra wide *bas* and so that's what he used to make for Ted. And then one day – it was a Thursday after school and Ted needed a new hurley for a game on the Saturday – we were outside this man's shed, hanging around, waiting for your man to finish Ted's hurley, when we saw this old radio transmitter, or that's what it looked like, thrown up against the wall.'

The sports pitch was out on the Dunmore road, on an elevated site, with views down over the island to the estuary.

'So Ted asked your man why he had thrown it out and your man said it was banjaxed. And that's how it all started. Ted gave him two shillings for the hurley and we went home with the new hurley and the wireless. It was some sort of a yoke that had been used by the British Army in the thirties and Ted said that your man had probably been able to listen to British naval exercises. Anyway, the next time I went up to Fowler Street, he had it working. All these valves and wires, but he had them figured out. He was a natural. I'd drop in to Fowler Street and he'd be up in his room, trying not to electrocute himself. The burns he used to get! One day I went in and he was listening to someone in fucking Moscow.'

Bobby tilted back his head and sighed.

'After that, when we left school and I started working in auctioneering for the Gargans, whenever we had a contents auction and there was any kind of a wireless in it, I used to always make sure it never went under the hammer. Gave it to Ted on the q.t. for spare parts. I can still see him, upstairs at the workbench. The size of his hands, and yet he was able to assemble these transmitters with all those tiny parts and wire and screws. God, I miss him.'

I thought of the three men in the old Flying Squad photograph.

'I was away in school when he died,' I said.

'He didn't die.' Bobby balled his fists. 'He was murdered. It was a fucking disgrace what happened. Unforgivable.'

I had heard passing references, as a teenager, to Uncle Ted's death, but no details. It had been as if the matter was too painful to be discussed, which in Waterloo particularly was how painful matters were dealt with.

'Ted didn't understand that in the North everything is divided. You only deal with your own group. So he bought a little van, began to make coal rounds. Kane's Coal, he called it. They painted warnings on the van. He took no notice. Ho-ho, he said, I'll be all right. They burned the van, but he bought another.'

The day began to slip away into the crimson western sky.

'They caught him down an alley on Christmas Eve. When he woke up in hospital, he was paralysed and blind. Iggy and Mags went to the police, but they were laughed at. Big strapping Ted who could carry a sack of coal on each shoulder. He lasted six months like that.' Bobby's lip quivered. 'Six months. I made the journey twice. The first time I brought them up meat the Gent gave me. Legs of lamb, loins of pork. The second time it was to bury him.' Bobby was panting. 'I'll tell you this much. Whatever Iggy does up there now, he's just defending himself.'

16

WATERFORD

December 1954

With Uncle Stanley and my father both dead, Granny Kane had switched her unquenchable need for worry on to Uncle Ted.

'I just wish he would come home for Christmas. I haven't seen them for nearly a year.'

'He has a farm to run, Mrs Kane,' said Bobby Gillece, now married to my Auntie Kate. 'A big responsibility.'

'My lovely little Iggy,' Granny said.

'Christmas is a busy time on a farm, Mother,' said the Gent, putting his cup and saucer aside. 'Labour goes home for Christmas.'

'He's after starting up a coal delivery business, Mrs Kane,' said Bobby, 'and Christmas is when all the money is made.'

'I know, I know, but why did he have to go so far away?' asked Granny, and sagged, as if the wind had gone out of her. 'If anything happens to him, how long will it take us to hear about it? He could be dead a week and still I wouldn't know.'

'We have a telephone being installed in the New Year, Mother,' said the Gent gravely, his foot tapping out its ceaseless message. 'I have one below in the office. If there is any news to be had, we'll get it straight away – isn't that right, Bobby?'

'Of course, we will,' Bobby said from his place beside the fire. 'All they have to do is lift the receiver and talk to the exchange. There's nothing to worry about, Mrs Kane.'

'And what about your poor mother and her farm?' Granny asked me, as if she had just remembered a fresh source of sadness. 'Oh, God, imagine, poor Paddy dead too.'

During the school holidays, Nancy always made sure I went to stay a night in Fowler Street.

'I'm going upstairs to lie down, Marty,' Granny said. 'Come and help me with those stairs.'

She was far heavier than she looked, as we made our way upwards, my arm around her. In her bedroom, she allowed me to ease off her shoes, and in a moment, she was asleep. As I tiptoed out to the head of the stairs, I could hear the men's low voices.

'Any word on that business?'

The Gent.

'My information is that so long as he stays away, there'll be no trouble. The guards have said as much,' Bobby replied.

'He's a right little cunt,' the Gent said. 'I never liked him.'

'He's my godson—'

'Godson my arse. What he did was in cold blood, to a mental retard, for fuck's sake.'

141

'He was only defending himself,' said Bobby in a wheedling voice, 'after what Stanley done to his kitten.'

'Defending himself? This is murder we're talking about! And anyway, poor Stanley couldn't dress himself, for fuck's sake, let alone do that to a cat.'

'Well then who did it?' Bobby asked. 'Huh?'

'Who do you think did it?' the Gent said. 'Little bastard, always up to mischief, looking for attention.'

'Ah, Jesus, that's harsh.'

'I saw him at it. "D'ye want sweets, Uncle Stanley? Say fuck the Gent and I'll give ye sweets!" I heard him, clear as I'm talking to you!'

'I know, that's a disgrace,' Bobby said. 'I gave him a couple of slaps myself, indeed I did. Spare the rod and spoil the child.'

'I never saw you except you were giving him thrupenny bits.'

'I chastised him too, I'm telling you.'

'Hmm,' said the Gent and I could almost see the look of scepticism on his face. 'If it wasn't for Ted, I'd fucking march him up to the barracks myself. He's a horrid little article. Nothing good will come of him, mark my words.'

Later, I lay down in Iggy's old bedroom where the radio sets had once been kept, fingering the two pound notes Granny had given me.

17

DUBLIN

September – October 1974

We are at our most primitive when it comes to death. We don't say dust to dust for nothing. We want to see our loved ones laid out, to kiss their icy foreheads, to touch their candled fingers and reassure ourselves that the cycle of birth and death remains intact. We lose our main co-ordinates if we don't see the coffin lid screwed on, or hear the roar of the furnace in the crematorium. Left without a body, we cannot truly mourn, for without a body we do not truly believe in death. We may appear to, but we don't. This is understandable, since death is essentially unimaginable. Without a body, we continue to clutch at the belief that life never ends, however absurd that possibility may be.

By the time autumn arrived I had made a decision. When Alison eventually called and asked me to meet her, I left the office early and drove into the Dublin Mountains.

'I came across a new adult toy in London last week,'

she said. 'It's a plastic square with coloured moving parts. You have to revolve the parts in order to align them all correctly. It's called a Rubik's Cube.'

'Did you succeed?'

'Eventually – after I persevered for most of the weekend. It just shows that success invariably requires patience.'

We were sitting in the snug of a little pub I had discovered, beyond Stepaside. Sugar was in England, part of a Fitzwilliam tennis team, and our children were in Waterloo with Fleming. I felt suddenly emboldened by my decision, as if I were somehow in charge of matters.

'There's a reason for everything, you know. Iggy Kane's father, my Uncle Ted, was crippled by Loyalist thugs in the North, probably because he was a Catholic trying to sell coal in Loyalist areas. The police ignored the incident. No wonder my cousin has problems with authority up there.'

Alison shook her head. 'What on earth has that got to do with murdering civilians in Britain?'

I took a deep breath. 'Look, I'm afraid I cannot become involved with what we last discussed. Not this time, not with him as the target. Sorry, but that is my decision.'

She made a point of drinking her whiskey. 'Is this some sort of joke?'

'I've never been more serious.'

'I see.'

'I'm sure you will understand.'

She sat unmoving, for almost a minute, and during that time her face became severely altered, in a way that was truly frightening, as if she was metamorphosing into another person before my eyes.

'And I had thought that you really were someone who

could make a difference,' she said so quietly I had to strain to hear.

Before I could respond, she had gathered her bag and coat and was on her feet.

'Alison, listen ...'

'You listen. We gave you an opportunity to make a meaningful contribution because we thought that was what you wanted. Personally, I have done my utmost to advance your career, and not without success. Now, at the first call to give something back, at a time of grave crisis, you welch. How very disappointing. And how very wrong I have been about you. Goodbye, Marty.'

Then she was gone, and I was left standing there, already empty and bereft.

I spent days in a kind of mental fever, like a gambler who, in a wild moment he will forever regret, has lost everything on a bad hand of cards. The fact that she was gone from my life – and that I had caused her to go – amazed me, for I had never until that moment grasped how much I relied upon her. It was not that she had been ever present in the physical sense, or that we had met more than once every couple of months, but nevertheless she had become the core of my working life. Everything I did in the Department, and how I did it, was ultimately informed by my arrangement with Alison. She had provided me with the meaning and excitement that I craved, but had not known I craved until I met her. Now, like someone sitting on a train that has broken down in the middle of nowhere, I felt powerless, defeated and depressed. It was as if the ten years gone by had all been a waste of time.

I tried to come to terms with the reason for my decision.

I wished that I could discuss my dilemma with someone, but there was no one. An elusive feeling of loyalty to my childhood seemed to be at the root of what governed me, which, as I went over it a hundred times, seemed more and more tenuous. I was letting my early memories of Waterford contaminate the clear-cut principles of justice that Alison, and I, stood for. The Iggy Kane I was trying to protect was no longer the companion whom I had yearned to be with all those years ago, but a cold-eyed killer who, for whatever reason, had decided his own fate. He had dominated me and manipulated my emotions throughout our childhood, and now, even though he could not have known it, was doing so again.

What would the Captain have thought? Despised Iggy Kane, without a doubt. The Captain had been a soldier, a man who had fought honourably and taken prisoners-of-war. He would have judged killing civilians as beneath contempt. I could hear myself reciting my predicament to him and imagine his derisive reaction.

Not my kind of chap.

I excused myself from our weekend trip to Waterloo, pleading an upcoming report that did not exist, and sat alone in Dublin like a man in the grip of a fatal disease. I wanted to drink myself into a state of insensibility, but knew that my situation would only be worse if I did so. Out on Sandymount Strand, in pouring rain, I actually contemplated walking out to sea and letting the tide look after my pathetic problems.

My terror was now centred on the probability that I had gone beyond the point of no return with her, and that for all I knew she might have packed up and returned to London, in which case I had fucked myself completely.

In sploshing shoes, I came home in darkness. My teeth chattered as I went straight to the phone. It rang and rang. I wanted to scream. She always answered on the first or second ring. I stood there, looking at myself in the hall mirror, a man gaunt, sodden, pale and terrified.

'Alison Chase.'

She seemed to be talking from thin air, but then I realised I was holding the phone down by my side.

'Alison,' I said. 'It's me.'

We never met twice in the same place, nor did we ever agree where we were going to meet until an hour or so before we did. It made sense to limit the possibilities of electronic eavesdropping, even then a rapidly evolving practise. Typical of the way our relationship had evolved, the location for the next meeting, when decided, sometimes by me, other times by her, always seemed to work. For example, that evening when I suggested a little pub on the Strawberry Beds, she said 'perfect' straight away.

We sat with whiskies and a bag of Tayto crisps, as if our previous encounter had never taken place.

'We're talking about the first Sunday in November. On that morning, in Armagh Cathedral, a young man called Joseph McGinn will be ordained a priest. You know who he is?'

I had to close my eyes in order to concentrate. 'I'm sure you're going to tell me.'

'He is the nephew of Ignatius Kane's stepmother, Margaret, or Mags, Kane. It will be a great occasion for the families; everyone will be invited. Including his cousin Marty.'

'How do you know that?'

'You will receive an invitation, believe me, as will Mr and Mrs Gillece. We've seen the guest list.'

It was as if I was having a dream in which I was forever drowning.

'That's only a few weeks away.'

'Exactly. Now we don't expect Kane to risk entering a confined space such as Armagh Cathedral, but we do think there's a good chance he'll attend the celebrations afterwards – especially if he knows that his favourite cousin Marty will be there.'

'I hate this.'

'It's as good an opportunity as we're likely to get,' she said. 'Are you all right?'

'You don't know that the celebrations, as you call them, will be held in the North,' I said and tried to take out a cigarette without shaking.

'That I acknowledge is a possible flaw – but as of this moment the McGinn family have reserved the banqueting hall of the Ramblers Inn, a couple of miles to the south-west of the town of Aughnacloy for that afternoon. But as you say, that could change, and if it does, then all bets are off.'

I was seized by terror, even as part of me did not believe what I had just been told. I bought more drinks, a double for myself, and more Tayto crisps, and we talked about politics and marriage, and our children. She could just breeze ahead, after what we had just discussed, without a bother, which was why her salary grade was, I assumed, far higher than mine.

It may seem odd now, but when I look back I cherish every moment of my meetings with Alison, even the awkward ones. For me it was like going time and again to a deep and unfailing well that ultimately sustained me. Her style was infectious. I cleaved to her for all my worth – I still do – and relegated such matters as my personal safety to a zone beneath my radar. I have always needed to be infatuated with someone, which I know says a lot about the elements of my character that are missing, but I don't care. I have always lived in turmoil, but I have always, in the main, been happy with the way I am.

'What exactly am I to do?' I asked eventually.

'Just turn up, Marty. Just turn up.'

'I'll be completely on my own up there, you know,' I said.

She smiled. 'Marty, you will not be on your own.'

18

DUBLIN

November 1974

Bill O'Neill had called me in. He was standing by the window to his office, his usual suit making a dark silhouette of him.

'How is the battle going?' he asked.

In conjunction with the recently formed Anglo-Irish Section, we were working on the wording of a proposal to try and rescue some elements of the failed Sunningdale Agreement, a tedious and depressing task, made all the more so by my inability to concentrate on such banalities at a time when I was caught up in plans for a foreign government-sponsored assassination.

'One step forward, two back,' I said. Framed black-and-white photographs, of what I assumed were Irish seascapes, filled the walls. Everything about Bill seemed monochromatic. 'You know the way.'

'To be sure I do.'

Bill sat behind his desk, invited me to take a chair and followed his usual ritual of tamping a pipe, which meant covering it with his hands, cracking a match in there, then sucking and puffing until overly sweet fumes filled the room like tear gas. He sat back with an air of general contentment. 'But there's a certain beauty to the whole process, isn't there? Like a courtship being conducted by way of correspondence, an almost eighteenth-century series of rituals and niceties. We move this way, they move that. Eyes upon each other. A smile every now and then, a touch, a meeting of minds. I can sometimes almost imagine a quill in my hand.'

Even though I had worked beside him for more than a decade, Bill was a man I knew little about. He was a bachelor. He sang in a male voice choir. He had entered the department with a degree in political science from UCD, but, other than that, as far as I was concerned, Bill might as well have come into the world like an egg.

'You're quite the romantic, Bill.'

He laughed, as if unused to compliments. 'Do you remember when you started work here at all? Years ago.'

I knew him well enough to know that he never asked a question lightly.

'Of course. I was interviewed by Seamus De Bárra and then handed over to you.'

'Ah, Seamus De Bárra, God be merciful to him. Did you know that he spent six years studying for the priesthood before he came in here?'

Small hands offering a chalice, came to my mind. A tinkling bike bell outside.

'I never knew that.'

'It goes to show that we can never predict where we'll end up, doesn't it? Take your own family. Years ago, you were all one down in Waterford. Now you're here in Dublin, and you've got cousins on the border. Who could have predicted that?'

He was busily tamping his pipe again.

'You're talking about Ignatius Kane's family,' I said.

'Well, his name does come up from time to time, yes.'

'Ah,' I said as darkness like a dull weight plunged in me, 'so you know about the ordination.'

'A great family occasion,' Bill said. 'Such days must be celebrated.'

'As a matter of interest, how did you... ?'

'No great secret. Telephone traffic is the job of our friends in the Gardaí and in military intelligence.'

I cursed myself. 'I should have told you, Bill, I'm sorry, but I didn't think there were security implications.'

'It's a young country and many of us have relations on both sides of the border,' Bill said, 'and we'd be much worse off if we didn't.'

'I apologise. I hope I haven't embarrassed you.'

'Me?' He took the pipe from his mouth. 'When I heard your name mentioned, I just let on that I had known all the time.'

I was being reproved, but then I saw a way out.

'I won't go,' I said with a flash of hope. 'In fact, now that you've put it into perspective, I can see how my presence might be viewed as inappropriate. And, again, I'm sorry for being so stupid.'

'Marty, Marty.' Bill shook his head. 'Have you learned nothing in all your time here?' He beheld me through vaporous tobacco. 'Of course you'll go.'

'I'll cry off, get a cold, have to be somewhere on business. It's much the best decision.'

'Please,' Bill said as his upper teeth were revealed. 'It's not everyone gets invited into that particular hinterland. And when you come back home, you'll be able to report every detail of what happened.'

19

WATERFORD – ARMAGH

November 1974

Dawn felt its way into the corners of the land. Bobby drove, both hands on the apex of the wheel. He smelled of strong, cheap cologne. You always got Bobby on such occasions, never Bobby and Auntie Kate. It was said that she refused to socialise with him because of his drinking, but Bobby's explanation was that someone had to stay at home and mind the pub. We crossed the border below Newry shortly after ten o'clock. Mirrors reflected from high towers. High above road blocks, Tommies in full camouflage with automatic weapons were inlaid in the starved setting. Beside a closed public house Bobby took out the sandwiches Auntie Kate had made, and a bottle of Powers Gold Label.

'Different country, boy,' he said more than once. 'Different people.'

I tried to put myself into Iggy's mind, arriving in this hinterland for the first time. Such starkness compared to

Waterford. Few friends, a new school, a new way of talking.

'When I was a kid, we used to dream of coming up here to fight,' Bobby said and picked at his false teeth with the car's ignition key. 'Of going to war up here. We had the guns, you know, oh yes, and your grandfather knew about it. We were hardy young fellas.'

'The Flying Squad,' I said.

He looked at me with surprise, as if something indelicate had suddenly appeared. 'How did you... ?'

'Iggy showed me the picture years ago,' I said. 'In Fowler Street.'

'Kids, we were just kids.'

I wanted to ask him who the third member of the trio with pistols was, but Bobby had changed the subject, and something about his expression told me to leave it.

'The Brits say the lads up here aren't soldiers but criminals. Fuck them! Look at Israel! Look at colonial America! Mark my words, one day the balaclavas will be wearing the suits, sitting around a table, discussing money and who gets what government portfolio.'

He poured whiskey into our glasses with excessive bonhomie. 'Harold Wilson wants to get to the core of things. Wants to walk out of Northern Ireland and turn the key, said as much. But he can't, so he'll have to sit down and talk to the lads, criminals or not.' Bobby's face became enlarged with excitement. 'I mean, this year they've already bombed Parliament – fuckin' Parliament!'

We moved north by way of high banks and stone walls, drenched cottages, the occasional bungalow with dormer windows, lanes that disappeared into hills. The little chink into the past that had opened for just an instant had closed again, like an oyster. Families filed into country churches of both denominations. Around a bend, the twin spires of the great cathedral suddenly sprang from the horizon.

20

Armagh

November 1974

Bishops and archbishops filled the high altar, as well as priests, deacons and altar-boys got out in white surplices. The men to be ordained knelt in a wide semi-circle. A choir resounded and crosses glittered. It was like attending the premier of an opera. Ten pews from the front, Bobby genuflected deeply, then slipped in and knelt for a minute, head in hands, the smell of drink off him now predominant. He sat back, whistling air, then nudged me and nodded his head towards the pew in front where two young neatly dressed men and two women in hats were seated.

'Ted's widow,' Bobby whispered.

Her face was long and heavily made up under a black straw hat. Her sons – Ted's sons, Iggy's half-brothers, both in their early twenties – wore dark suits. One of them was cleanly shaven with neat fair hair; the other had a heavy red beard. Beside them, sitting awkwardly, was a hatless woman, heavily pregnant, her dark hair already turning grey. Jennifer, Iggy's wife.

Bobby leaned forward.

'Mrs Kane?'

Four sets of eyes turned around.

'Bobby Gillece from Waterford, how are you? And this is Marty Ransom.'

She stared at Bobby and then smiled broadly.

'You made it!' she cried. 'Boys! Look! Your cousins from Waterford are here!'

We weaved north-west, hugging the border, as the evening began to close in. A motionless column of smoke stood on the roof of a whitewashed cottage half-a-mile away. Ahead of us, the Kane brothers drove their mother and Iggy's wife, who, I had learned, was due to give birth before Christmas. At least four other cars, carrying the newly ordained priest and his extended family, followed behind. I had seen no soldiers, no police in the church, but they had been there, I knew, not just the plainclothes stooges from the UK Special Branch, or case officers from MI5, but also the handlers from Dublin who were at home on this beat, men planted in the local communities. I put my head back and became detached in the way I always did in the presence of danger. My ears closed. I hated what I was doing. And yet women in England had been murdered on buses.

'The new priest is a right character, isn't he?' Bobby chortled.

Earlier, we had all stood outside the cathedral for photographs. The thin wind had made the women shiver, but I had seen the way the Kane lads had looked at one another when they heard how I spoke. And when I had asked them how Iggy was, they had turned away, as if my saying his name aloud in such a setting confirmed their worst suspicions.

'Where in the name of God are they bringing us at all?' Bobby asked.

A cold river below us snaked through wet farmland, snipe grass, stark straggles of gappy hedges. Steep dark hills to our right. The river was the border between Ireland's separate jurisdictions and much of this terrain was no-man's land.

I hated what I was doing, and because of that I suddenly hated Alison, something I had not previously thought possible. Of course, as I had read in some worthy journal, the person I really hated was myself, for, just as all the characters in our dreams are different manifestations of ourselves, so the objects of our deepest abhorrence are trapped in the parts of us that have fallen into the lost abyss of our souls.

I was mostly deaf, and my fearful, milky vision of the road ahead kept leaping in and out as I recalled the descriptions of what had been found after some of the explosions. A man's finger with a wedding band attached. Body matter like tripe stuck to broken windscreen glass.

And yet... and yet Iggy Kane was part of our family, my father's nephew, and the rules for families are unlike any other rules. Despite despising Iggy for what he had done, and was continuing to do, my father would have appreciated that someone linked to him by blood came into a different category. Especially the only son of Uncle Ted, the brother he had loved. He might decide to give Iggy a final warning, or make an exception. He might well draw the line when it came to such an extreme act as I was involved in. I realised with a sickening jolt that however minuscule the possibility, there still existed a chance that my father might one day reappear, and if he did, I would have to explain how I had lured his brother's son to his death.

I decided to crash the car: to lurch sideways into Bobby, grab the steering wheel, ram it hard over and plunge us into the river. I would be killed, but I didn't care. Bobby too. But what if we didn't die? If the car merely slid pathetically into the current and we had to crawl out with bruises and other injuries? Or we were rescued, cut from the wreckage by firemen and brought by ambulances to Armagh? Bobby, if he survived, would report on what I had done. *The fucker tried to kill us both! I knew years ago he couldn't be trusted!* On the other hand, I could probably, with luck, drown him, that's if we made it into the river, but the people in the cars behind might see me doing it. Or, looking on the bright side, during the crash, Bobby might be convulsed by the heart attack he was widely expected to suffer, go blue with terror as we nose-dived, suck for air, gasp his last. Was there a steeper incline to pitch us over? I could see the river clearly and my breath came in great gasps.

'Marty? Wake up! We're here.'

Chippings popped under our tyres. The car park was set down like a viewing point above the river, a platform from which to inspect the misty fields and tiny hills of the Republic. Members of Iggy's family were already assembled, smiling, as if proximity to the border was a happy thing.

'How will we ever find our way home?' Bobby asked, even as it was clear that he didn't care.

The walls of the Ramblers Inn were painted livid green and a tricolour fluttered above the gable. Other cars were pulling in now, and parking, but besides our group, I could see no one else. I was seized by a burst of hope: he had decided not to come. Bobby locked the car and said, 'I'd give my eye-teeth for a half-one.'

With a hearty cheer, the priest was lifted shoulder high by the young lads and we began to walk towards the pub. Approaching the gable with its defiant flag, as my universe telescoped crazily on the pub door, as I wondered if, for once, Alison had got the day wrong, Iggy stepped from the shadows.

Within the next few, infinitely elastic seconds I lived several lives. His face had not changed, in fact he could still have been the same boy – same square head and prominent cheekbones, same probing eyes that were now examining and re-examining every inch of the car park – but he had put on weight and his suit, including a waistcoat, was too small for him. His hair, longer than I remembered, licked over his ears. Good shoes. He took a step. I pushed to the fore. He was speaking to me. Saying something. His half-smile. What right had he to be so happy? And me? I had achieved small but significant advances for my country, albeit by unconventional means. Even as I fought to keep going, I was trawling at speed over the hundreds of times we had been together, and talked and played, and made ourselves the heroes of our games, with rules and codes and tricks to outwit our enemies.

'Marty.'

I halted. For Iggy alone, I drew two fingers across my throat, like a pirate.

Time snapped. Iggy stopped dead. His blue eyes. To my right, at a distance of no more than five hundred yards, I could suddenly see the revolving blades. To someone of lesser height, they might not have been visible, but I could now make out the blur of a rotor.

Iggy was already running back towards the pub. Men I hadn't seen appeared, at least one with a handgun. A cry from Jennifer, Iggy's pregnant wife. The priest said, 'Is there something...?'

The roar. Two Lynxes – huge – rose from the earth and swung in at us, noses down, like gigantic moths. Harnessed soldiers dangled in mid-air, weapons cradled. From the same direction, two camouflaged armoured personnel carriers and an RUC vehicle had burst to life.

'Oh, no,' I heard Auntie Mags say.

Rifle fire caused one of the helicopters to bank sharply. The goggles of the gun crews. From behind the pub a jeep that had been parked out of sight hurtled for the river. The Kane boys were on their knees, hands behind their heads, surrounded by RUC men. Jennifer was steering Auntie Mags back to their car. Alone and bewildered, the newly ordained Father Joseph McGinn looked lost. Iggy's jeep had forded the river and disappeared. The Lynxes hovered impotently between the public house and the border, as though a pane of glass prevented them from flying further. All at once the car park was full of policemen. A cordon of soldiers had formed an outer perimeter.

Part III

Part III

1

WATERLOO

December 1974

Waterloo was never more beautiful than in winter. For reasons I never fully came to terms with, all my best memories of the Captain were set in those lovely crisp dawns when the foothills stood out like marquetry. Years later, I could still hear his feet on the wooden stairs, and the squeak of the back door, and was seized by an overwhelming need to be with him, my arm linked through his as we met the rising ground that led, either to the ridge, or, if we went left, into a series of large fields that plummeted into the valleys. Along the headland, the hedgerows were tinselled elaborately with spiders' webs. As I cocked my ear for tumbling larks, a skein of geese flowed like a miracle of dark ink across the pale morning sky.

By a gate, where an old horse plough had been abandoned, the Captain took out cigarettes and snapped one alight. My nostrils dilated. The sun began to inch into the fields as crows hopped between the grass tufts. In a clump of gorse, just for an instant, the gliding white tip of a vixen's brush was visible. My father tucked me into him and we forged on, heads dipped into a sudden wind. His tweed sports coat had leather elbow patches and his dark hair was slicked flat with Morgan's Pomade, whose leathery scent had become a part of him. I didn't care about going home for breakfast. I would happily have starved out there if it could have meant us staying together.

One such lovely morning, in bed, I reached over to fondle the neck of my wife and she turned away. Ten minutes later we were standing, face to face, me with fists clenched, she with tears running down her face.

'How long has this been going on?'

'Oh, what does it matter?' she said. 'Six months, if you must know.'

'Who is he?'

'You don't know him. He's a businessman – he lives in Dublin. He's married.'

'I suppose he plays tennis.'

'So what if he does? I listen to what he tells me; he listens to me. We talk, we talk, we talk.'

At least we were in Waterloo, where the thick walls meant that such scenes could be conducted with discretion. I watched Sugar's outline through her nightgown as she drew back the curtains, shook out a cigarette, flamed her lighter and sucked deeply. Birdsong rang out with harmonious irony; the hooves of Emmet's pony echoed from the stable yard.

'It's my fault,' I said. 'I know it is.'

'We've been through it all, Marty, so many times. I

just don't know you, that's the problem, and it terrifies me. I haven't a clue what's going on inside you, or where that thing, whatever it is, is taking you. It's as if I'm being continually deceived.'

'So your response was to deceive me.'

'There's a difference between unfaithfulness and deception. At least I've told you. You never tell me anything.'

My mind kept flying to all that I stood to lose when she left me, as I now knew she would, even knowing at the same time that her decision would be the right one for her and our children.

'If he's going to leave his wife, and since he can't divorce her here, he'll probably have to move to England. Is that your plan, too?'

'He won't leave his wife. We're just two people who have collided in the dark.'

'You make it sound like the dodgems.'

'It's not sex I'm looking for! It's warmth, it's friendship. So if intimacy with another man is the price for me to try and be happy, then so be it!'

'I'm sorry for my shortcomings, but I don't think I deserve to be cuckolded because of them.'

'Have you any idea what it's like for me? I'm living with a stranger! You've become a caricature of the man I married, going through the motions, driving up and down to Dublin, pretending to farm – but all the time it's as if there's another person there, in your job, doing whatever it is you do, that you won't tell me about. Jesus, for all I know you could be murdering people and I wouldn't know it!'

'Sugar ...'

'Shut up, please.' She stubbed out her cigarette and,

wrapping her gown tightly, wiped away her tears with the back of her hand.

'The children and I are going to live with my mother in Carlow,' she said. 'Fleming is coming with us.'

2

DUBLIN

December 1974

It pained me most at weekends, on my way south, to drive within a mile of the house in Carlow. I once parked on the grass verge near the entrance, hoping I might see them, but then realised how much to type my position was, and how my wife might interpret it if she found me. Even worse, I realised, as I drove off, would have been to see her happy with her new man, or to see him with my children. The extent to which I had ruined my life was never clearer. And all for what? I had betrayed my employers, and I had betrayed my wife. And although I considered what I was doing to be in the interests of my country, no one else would see it like that. At nights, on my own, in Waterloo, I often drifted off to sleep soothed by a fond image of my father drinking a gin and tonic and regaling pretty girls with one of his stories. Sometimes he was in Buenos Aires, sometimes in sub-Saharan Africa. He was not yet sixty, but his hair had gone grey, and he had become thin with age, but the vitality I remembered was still there, and unless you knew him, you would never know that this old man had walked out of another life.

In one of the new coffee shops that had begun to sprout around the edges of the city – this one on the north side – a wheezing sound system played a loop of Christmas music.

'I'm so sorry this has happened,' she said.

'She's in Carlow, with her mother. I send her every penny I can afford. Her mother's a bitch who makes it impossible for me to visit.'

I had been to see my solicitor in Waterford, Dick Coad, who ran his practice in rooms over a shop in Gladstone Street. Dick, a man whose eyes seemed to rotate in unaligned orbits, advised me that, in his experience, if the fondness of the heart survived even minutely, then so, eventually, did the marriage.

'Remember years ago in Waterloo when we spoke about how strange it would have been if Sugar had married Christopher?' I asked Alison. 'We wondered what you and I would have done. I sometimes think it might have been better, because I'm married to Sugar but I'm also married to you.'

'You love her, Marty.'

'But she's not able to love me as I am. She knows what I'm doing, you know.'

Alison's eyebrows rose fractionally. 'You told her?'

'Of course I didn't tell her. She can smell it off me.' I shuddered. 'Look, I need out.'

Alison shook her head sympathetically. 'I know, Marty. I know.'

'I have nothing,' I said. 'I've lost those I love. I'm dying.'

'I know.'

'Really?'

'So I'm ending it. Effective now,' she said.

'Are you serious?'

'Absolutely. The decision has been made.'

'What...does that mean?'

'It means you and I shan't be available any more to help each other in political matters.'

'But...'

'Yes, Marty, we are still friends, of course we are. We will always be friends.'

Despite this being what I wanted most, I felt the cut of loss. We had reached the same point that we had arrived at several months before, but in this case, by agreement.

'You're not going back to London, then.'

'Of course not – or at least, not yet. Look, there are many ways that friends can keep in touch.'

Mysteriously, I was transported back in that instant to the hammock in Waterloo, and the feel of her warm thigh, and the attendant rush of fear and excitement that I had felt then.

'You'll get used to it,' she was saying. 'I suggest you wait a few months to get acclimatised, then go back to Sugar. You'll have nothing to hide – you'll no longer smell of it, to use your expression.'

'Does Vance know? I realise that's a stupid question.'

She smiled. 'Vance really likes you and probably envies you.'

'He once told me I was a very lucky man. He was talking about Sugar.'

She picked up a knife and sliced a Danish pastry in two. 'You've made a very significant contribution, something we greatly appreciate – and it's been positive for everyone. At the same time, we understand the finite nature of these arrangements. There's no point in you being miserable, living apart from Sugar, whom you adore, your lovely Emmet and Georgie. Nurse Fleming.'

'I can get by without Fleming.'

'However,' she poured tea into the cheap white cups, 'I need to know what exactly happened in south Armagh. Our people are furious but mystified. Can you throw any light on why he may have bolted?'

I had prepared for this in the weeks that had gone by since the incident. 'I'm not sure,' I said and met her steady gaze. 'He came out of the pub and when he saw me he ran for it.'

'Which, if true, makes our involving you a farce.'

'Why didn't you take him out before I arrived?'

'Because we didn't have a visual. The pub is two hundred yards from the border. We didn't know he was in there for sure until he emerged. Our people did a positive ID and relayed it to Special Ops, but by then he was on the move.'

'It was an idiotic plan in the first place. Imagine if you'd killed the priest.'

She sighed. 'Perhaps it was foolish. The impression is, however, that something tipped him off. Or someone. You probably have a fair idea of the amount of work involved in an operation like this. Thing is, it very nearly worked, but something happened.'

'He obviously saw the danger – saw your people. Or heard the choppers.'

'No.' She was adamant. 'He got a signal. Did you see anything?'

I felt a surge of relief. 'Nothing. I saw him. I was walking towards him. He was saying something to me. Then he started running back towards the pub.'

'Your in-law – Bobby? Might he have warned him?'

'I don't think so,' I said with a spike of glee. 'Although Bobby was walking behind me, so perhaps he did – who knows?'

She began to pick up crumbs with her fingers. 'We don't know how Ignatius Kane became aware of us and we probably never will. The shame is that he'll kill another couple of dozen innocent people before we get our next chance.' She sat back. 'But now it's over for you.' I wondered then was there anyone in my life I had not at some point betrayed, Alison included.

'Aren't you glad that you're out of this ghastly business, Marty?'

'What about you? Are you out of here, too?'

'Not till next year, or the one after that – then I'm away! Like a kite! Or an enormous balloon! I may sail over you one day in Waterloo. You'll be sitting outside with Sugar, drinking wine by the lake, and all of a sudden one of your beautiful children will rush over, pointing into the sky and shrieking, "Daddy, Daddy! Look up! It's Alison!"'

3

DUBLIN – WATERFORD

January – March 1975

At first, my new world was a novelty. My loyalty, now exclusively at the disposal of Iveagh House, felt not just strange, but difficult, a puzzle in itself, for one would have assumed that serving one master was less demanding than answering to two. As time wore on, my working day, once a tightrope on which I had effortlessly performed, was revealed in all its banality, and I realised just how dull were the lives of my colleagues, how blunt compared to the razor's edge on which I had previously balanced. I was one of them now, a civil servant with a family, although mine had fled, whose soul hid nothing more than the venal thoughts of ordinary men. On the other hand, I could sleep without fear of what I might babble in a dream. My heart no longer leapt.

I had described for Bill O'Neill the events I had been part of in south Armagh in exactly the same way I had described them for Alison. The ordination, the procession to the pub, the appearance of Iggy Kane. I gave Bill the names of all the people in our group, including Iggy's family and the priest's. Given the information that I knew Bill was being fed by the army and Gardaí, he would surely have known already about the events at the Ramblers Inn, but although he listened to me amiably, and took detailed notes, he never commented, except to make sympathetic noises when I described the terrifying climax outside the pub. Where exactly Bill's allegiances lay was never clear to me; he was a complex man. For all I knew, he could well have been briefed in advance of the south Armagh operation.

One day he put his head around my door. 'Charlie's back,' he said with a grin.

After five years in the political wilderness, my old friend Mr Haughey had just been appointed shadow spokesman for Health and Social Welfare. His disgrace and fall from office six years previously had been put aside and left to history.

'Maybe this time he'll behave himself,' I said.

'This time he'll go all the way to the top,' Bill said. 'No one will stop him now.'

I had never heard Bill express an opinion on an Irish politician before, but Haughey had a way of drawing even the most neutral of men to his forward march. Thereafter, on several occasions, I gave Bill the opportunity to discuss in more detail what had happened in south Armagh, to make a comment, or ask a question about the particular hinterland I had entered, in an effort to determine what exactly he knew, but he never bit. He puffed his pipe and we discussed whatever political common ground existed in Northern Ireland

175

as a way of defusing the crisis that had engulfed the province.

In Bobby Gillece's pub the smoke sat at eye level. Our excursion together to south Armagh seemed to have created a new bond between us, as it does between fellow soldiers who have seen action together. From Bobby's point of view, he and I had been the targets of a British Army ambush, which had at last put us on the same side, and confirmed for Bobby that all his old suspicions and political allegiances were justified. He had inflated his own role outside the Ramblers Inn into a near heroic escapade with which his customers had already become weary.

'The news from Iggy is not good,' he said to me from the side of his mouth.

'Oh?'

'Their baby was born a week ago.' The bones in Bobby's jaw popped. 'A girl. Poor little thing has a hole in her heart.'

Notwithstanding our new camaraderie, my security lay in staying close to Bobby, for if Iggy suspected that my warning to him had arisen, not from my spotting the helicopters, but from a loss of nerve, then he would tell Bobby, and Bobby, I was sure, would be unable to conceal it from me.

'Not fair, is it?' he said. 'They've waited so long and this is what they get. The doctors say she won't live.'

'Sometimes I think this God of ours is a monster.'

Bobby looked at me in surprise, then his bottom lip curled out. He reached his hand towards me and I realised he was drunk.

'Can I tell you something?'

'Sure, Bobby.'

He had a grip on me. 'I think about you a lot. An awful lot.'

The discomfort I had sometimes felt as a child in Fowler Street when he was around now crawled over me.

'We've known each other a long time,' I said.

'I know, but ...' He gasped. 'You see ...'

'It's all right, Bobby, it's fine.'

'You see, I was there that day, on the quay,' he said. 'I saw what happened.'

'What are you talking about?'

'The day you took the boat to England, to go to school. I saw you on the quay with her.'

'With who?' I asked.

'With Kate,' Bobby sobbed. 'Do you not remember?'

4

WATERLOO FARM – WATERFORD

September 1952

Cattle stretched in shade as mallard beat the lake into a frenzy. By the front door, Oscar slept, twitching, occasionally lunging at a fly. Eileen, who had been there since I was born, and for whom every year of the last twelve had been tainted with dread for this moment, stood in her apron, grinding her hands. In my correctly creased grey flannel short pants and tweed sports coat, I was all at once so much taller than she was. Eileen had been persuaded not to make the journey to Waterford.

'You don't have to come either, Paddy,' Nancy said. She threw down her cigarette and swivelled on it with her heel.

'Some things I need to get in town,' the Captain said. 'Come on!'

I clicked my tongue at Oscar, who sat up to have his ears rubbed. I wondered if he would still sleep on the old horse blanket at the foot of my bed. Danny stood at some distance.

'See you at Christmas, Danny!'

Danny had vivid notions about English women that he had been sharing with me ever since he had heard where I was being sent to school. The Morris gurgled and fumes seeped out from beneath its chrome fender. There was a brief, awkward fumbling with Eileen, then I climbed into the back seat with my wooden trunk, last used in the Transvaal by my maternal grandfather. Eileen at the car window, the Captain staring straight ahead. Nancy revved the engine and we lurched forward.

'Christ, that bloody woman drives me mad,' the Captain grumbled as we shot past the lake.

A cloud shadow moved across the mountain. The car backfired, twice, and Harry, my pony, made high, indignant steps across the paddock. That morning I had fed him oats, normally reserved for hunting days, and had later ridden him, flat out, in the big, triangular field. I felt odd now, dressed in the proper clothes required by my new school; for the previous twelve years I had worn hand-me-downs from Fowler Street, and only occasionally clothes purchased from Our Boys in Dublin, when the Captain was flush.

He was not flush any more. A slowness had entered the way he walked, or confronted bad news, or got up from his armchair. It was as if his ever-precarious financial situation had ground him down, leaving behind only a marooned grandiosity. In his study one night, when he had gone to bed, I found a letter he had written to his brother Ted, asking for the loan of five pounds. It was signed, 'Your loving brother, Paddy'. His trips to England were made to escape his creditors, I had realised that summer when a decent trout from the lake had often meant the difference between supper or not. I had put on his old khaki shorts and tennis shoes and waded out waist deep with a net tacked between two poles. Soon, my shoulders, back and chest were the colour of harness leather and my hair hammered into copper.

I kept glancing back to see Waterloo shrinking beneath me. Even though I accepted the decision that had been made to send me away, and was even looking forward to it, I still wondered why Iggy could attend the Christian Brothers in south Armagh, now his home, while I had to go to England.

The angle of my mother's cigarette seldom changed. When the ash grew perilously long, she wound down the car window and flicked it out. She now handed back her Craven 'A' to me, and the metal lighter that had once been her father's. I took out a cigarette, flamed it alight and inhaled.

'If you're going to smoke, you need a decent lighter,' she said. 'I'll buy you one for Christmas.'

'How is he going to afford to smoke aged twelve?' the Captain asked.

'He can smoke mine,' my mother said and threw her eyes to heaven.

She was tense in a way I had not noticed before, whether because formerly she had not been tense, or whether I had become more attuned than I used to be, I could not say. The Captain had lost part of his flamboyance and I think that irritated her. I had become gradually aware that she was an attractive woman; when she walked down the Quay, men turned their heads.

Suddenly the twinkling river mouth, always exciting,

edged into view. The Captain was rattling on about clubs in London, and how, if there wasn't another war – this time with Russia – he would be over to visit me. 'I'm too old to fight, but you might have to,' he said.

'He will *not* fight!' Nancy snapped and her tone was so unusual that his head went back as if she'd slapped him.

The ever-changing shades and hues seemed to consume us in our descent to the town. A boots was polishing the door brasses of the Granville Hotel as we passed the Clock Tower and pulled up at the customs shed on Adelphi Quay.

'Russia is not Ireland's argument, thank God,' Nancy said and switched off the engine.

'Oh shit,' said the Captain.

Auntie Kate and Auntie Angela were standing on either side of Granny Kane, who was perched on an upright chair. My grandmother wore her customary black, but Auntie Kate's light summer frock was being pressed into her legs by the breeze.

With his English-sounding name, rank and ways, his never-explained sources of income, his sudden disappearances and reappearances, his social connections and ostentatious approach to life my father had become someone whom the Kanes neither understood nor approved of. Even though his mother would never have criticised him in public, and was proud that he had fought a war, she was hurt by the fact that he had distanced himself from his natural family.

Nancy, grasping the awkwardness of the situation, rushed forward to kiss all the women and then thrust me at them, as the Captain stood, hands behind his back, and made remarks to no one in particular about the weather and the perfect sailing conditions.

'Kate, stand beside Martin,' said Auntie Angela, who was peering into a Box Brownie. I don't think I had ever heard her speak more than two words before. 'Stand still, both of you.' Auntie Kate wrapped her arm around my waist. 'Lovely!' cried Auntie Angela.

I turned to heft out my trunk.

'Oh, God,' I heard the Captain say.

'Marty. Come over here now!'

My mother was beckoning. The steamer let out a short hoot. Granny Kane's eyes were large with tears. 'You're going to break all the girls' hearts, including mine,' she said.

'I'll be back at Christmas, Granny.'

She was never far from desolation, but the proximity of the Captain, now chatting to Auntie Kate in his courtly, unconcerned way, made the old woman set her jaw.

'This is for you, love.' She put her hand into mine. 'Put it in your pocket quickly,' she whispered and held me close.

'Thank you.' I stole a glance at the Captain, but he was now looking over the vessel like a visiting admiral.

'We'll miss you,' Granny said.

The boat hooted again. Auntie Angela, head down, offered me her cheek. I had to walk around a stack of pallets to get to the gangplank.

'Marty?'

I stopped.

'Do I not get one?' asked Auntie Kate.

We were hidden by the pallets. She turned me, so that she was facing the ship, and clamped her hands to my head as she brought her face to mine. Her most delicious tongue sprang into my mouth and fed there. Over her shoulder, I suddenly saw the Captain approaching, eyes narrowed. I was gasping. My father stuck out his hand.

'I envy you, boy,' he said. 'I'd give anything to play some proper rugger again.' The corner of his mouth twitched and the old wolfish glint was briefly evident. 'Keep your flies buttoned, you hear me?'

The bones in my ears hummed. Auntie Kate's taste was like treasure I wanted to hoard and gloat upon. Nancy too was now beside me, her expression distraught.

'Bye, Mum.'

'You ... ' Her face was awash. 'You are the light and meaning of my life. Do you understand that?'

I heard her words but they meant little. She glowed as she held me out from her. I wondered if I should kiss them all again, including Auntie Kate.

'Do you hear me?'

'Yes, Mum.'

She gripped me tight. The porter was waiting with my trunk and then I was in the customs shed, answering questions about where I was going and why.

'He's Pa Kane's grandson,' the porter told the customs officer.

Seized by love, which now sat within me as a deep and cruel need right at the moment when it could not be satisfied, I stood on the suddenly moving deck of the steamer. The Kanes were huddled together, Auntie Kate to her mother's right. My mother was by the Morris, one foot on the running board. The Captain was sitting in the car. Waterford began to shrink as the boat forged into mid-stream. Cormorants, erect as sentries, lined the mud banks. The Quay was like a broad hem on the base of the receding, cascading town. I could see my mother waving beyond seagulls as they screeched over the churning wake. As we entered the mid-stream, the ridges of Bally-bricken appeared. In my pocket I touched what Granny Kane had made me stuff there. I took out two five-pound notes. Giddily, I stared at them. I looked back again, but the town was lost in haze. The boat's engines thundered. Gradually, the banks fell away as the land became less significant and we forged our course towards the sea.

5

WATERFORD

March 1975

Bobby squirmed and for a most uncomfortable moment I thought he was going to try to kiss me.

'Your grandmother had asked me to go aboard and make sure you had the best cabin.'

Outlandishly, after so long, I could still respond to the memory of his wife's tongue with a degree of longing.

'I grew up next door to the ship's captain. He insisted I go on to the bridge for a half-one. We had a bottle downed when I looked out the porthole and saw you and Kate.'

I sat back. 'Bobby, with the greatest respect, that was almost twenty-five years ago. And you weren't even married.'

'We were engaged. She was wearing my ring. But, look, you were only a boy...' He shook violently and looked as if he might be about to cry again. 'I never said anything to her. I was...I was afraid she'd...I didn't want to lose her...'

And then he did cry with big, noisy gulps, into his sleeve, unable to look at me.

'After that ... even though we were married ... we never ... Every time I tried ... I never could ...'

'It's all right, Bobby, it's all right.'

'I would have loved children,' he sobbed. 'I would have loved a little girl.'

A week later, I rang Sugar from the Royal Hotel in Carlow. An hour later, she sat across from me in the hotel's wood-panelled bar.

'I want you to come home. I won't bore you by apologising again, except to say that I have taken certain measures. You will find me changed. My mind is clear. I'm a free man, truly free. Everything you did was understandable. I would have done the same, I'm sure. What is easy for some men is difficult for me, something I didn't realise when I was getting into all this. But I can't live without you, because I love you. Give me one more chance.'

She looked at me for such a long time that I thought it really was over. But then she reached across and took my hand. 'I will, Marty,' she said.

Her mother never appeared the next day, a minor blessing. Later, at home, Sugar told me that part of the reason she had decided not to leave me permanently was that her late father, Canon Ferguson, had always spoken of me in terms of affection. Even when she had despaired of me, he had insisted that she try and see my good side. I said a quiet prayer of thanks to that country rector. He had also served two masters on the battlefield, God and man, which made us more alike than he could have ever known.

Sugar and I resumed our lives in Dublin and Waterloo, although since Emmet went to school in Dublin, Waterloo was thought more of as a place for holidays. We never discussed the Dublin businessman, as if he had not existed, somewhat like the work I had left behind. Sugar came to me in bed without restraint, and told me one morning, when I mentioned the need for caution, that when we'd been separated she'd gone and had her tubes tied. I was flabbergasted.

'Why?'

'Because I wanted my children to be only yours.'

Why I should have felt deprived, I'm not sure, since she was depicting her action as having been made out of love for me, but I did. On the other hand, I had to balance this information with the numerous acts I had been involved in, and kept from her, over almost a decade, although none seemed as personal as a tubal ligation. I was not aware that I had wanted more children, but now the choice had been made for me.

From Sugar's point of view, my new dispensation, which is how I privately thought of it, was a success. It took me time to realise that I had nothing to hide, in the same way I had read how those who defeat the urge to suicide suddenly realise that there is nothing to despair. For a while I could imagine myself back as the carefree young farmer, living in his hilly outpost, his life stretching before him, just as the bounty of the land stretched into the distance beneath Waterloo.

I bought a second-hand Land Rover, and a cob for Emmet. He and I shot rabbits in the foothills, and went to the seashore at Benvoy, outside Tramore, and once caught a sea bass off the rocks.

6

WATERLOO – DUBLIN

January 1976

I know exactly when I felt the tug. It was on Christmas Day in Waterloo, carving the goose, my wife and children and Nurse Fleming all wearing party hats, a decanter of wine glowing from the table, hoar frost on the window glass, the yawning presence of our mountain all around us. It took me over quickly, in less than a minute, sucked my breath from my chest and left me weak. I had to concentrate on the glistening bird flesh beneath my hands in order not to show my family that I had been seized by a primal craving.

Over the days that followed, I put my condition down to an excess of well-being, something every man experiences from time to time, and tried to deal with it in bed with my wife. In early January, the weather turned rainy and I read books to regulate my mind, not that I disapproved of masturbation, but because masturbation did not work. The images became so insistent in their detail that every time I drank a whiskey I could see her face. How was this possible, I reasoned, when I was married to a beautiful woman without inhibitions? With whom I was deeply in love? The mother of my children?

Even more puzzling was that, in our years of working together, I had never fantasised about her with such force, or seriously considered calling in the ancient promise she'd made on that faraway summer's day. Nor had I essentially regarded her as other than a colleague with whom I was doing necessary, albeit irregular, work. Now I couldn't rid myself of…I couldn't even say it. It was as if I now needed her in a different way. Was I in love with her? How could I be? Making love to Sugar, I saw Alison's perfect face, her knowing brown eyes; even as I bestrode my wife's trim body, I yearned for Alison's bulk.

It was as if by the subtraction of the tasks she had formerly set me, whether in the simple relaying to her of classified information, or the more complex interactions she had designed with meticulous attention to detail, a want had been created in me that only she could satisfy. So used had I become to living in the shadow, that now, out in the sun, the direct light was more than I could bear. Simply, I was sick for the want of her. All in all, I suppose, a rather pathetic way of trying to explain why, one Monday in mid-January, I rang her.

7

County Wicklow, Ireland

January – June 1976

As I approached the cottage, I felt an apprehension far greater than I'd ever felt when I had reason to be fearful, for my adultery had not yet taken place and I was simply on the way to meet an old family friend. Part of my anxiety was without foundation, but nonetheless centred on Iveagh House finding out that I was having an affair with, or about to have an affair with, a high-ranking official in the British Embassy, as if they would somehow find more to disapprove of in a sexual than in an intelligence betrayal.

The address to which she had directed me was in a county I knew little, a mile outside a village I'd never been to. I had no idea whose house it was, or if she used it often. Rainwater spilled from the gutter and ran down the faded brickwork. Someone had left a wheelbarrow of weeds on the lawn the previous summer, where it now stood, drenched and rotten. Her car was parked around the side. I rang the bell.

Light spilled down the hall as the front door was opened. She seemed, as always, to know exactly what I needed, for she stepped towards me and in an instant we were kissing with abandon. I'm not proud of this, but I'm not ashamed of it either. As if we'd spent our whole lives waiting, we lurched, half-entwined, upstairs, dropping clothes as we went, and made as one for the large double bed that filled almost the entire space at the upper level.

Later, as we drank tea, a cat that must have climbed the trellis outside was sitting on the sill of the bedroom window. 'It must have seen everything,' I said, and we laughed.

'Don't you like cats?'

In so many ways she was like a cat: calculating, pleasure-seeking and ultimately quite dangerous.

'We never had cats,' I said. 'I mean in Waterloo. But I remember them in Fowler Street. Iggy liked them.'

She looked at me in mild surprise, as if I'd broken a fundamental rule. I got out cigarettes and we smoked them with an ashtray between us, until eventually I could take the cat's scrutiny no more and went and shooed it away.

'You're full of surprises,' she murmured as I returned to bed. She ran her finger over an old scar on my rib cage. 'Looks like you were tortured. Were you?'

'Sort of.'

'Kenya?'

'Collateral damage.'

'We are all damaged in some way, aren't we?'

She told me that the cottage belonged to a cousin of Christopher's, a woman who lived in London and owned an art gallery. She seldom came to Ireland and had given Alison and Christopher the key.

'Where is Christopher?' I asked, as if he came under the heading of damage.

Alison snorted. 'Back in London. Has been for nine months.'

'I didn't know.'

'How could you?'

'Is he...? Are you divorcing?'

'I'm not sure if I can be bothered, to be honest, and I dare say he lacks the energy in that as in all other things.'

'He had a job here.'

'Even Whitehall cannot persuade a commercial bank to indefinitely employ an incredibly ineffective, lazy man. He's trying to get into some sort of consultancy or other. How is Sugar?'

'Very well, thanks.' I started another cigarette. 'My mother died last month.'

'I know, I'm sorry,' Alison said. 'I didn't know whether I should mention it.'

'Why would you not?'

'None of my business, is it?'

I looked at her. 'You English really are different to us.'

'Maybe in some ways,' she said and licked my ear, 'but not in others.'

'I'm glad of that.'

I had never met anyone like her, which of course had always been the case, but the impression was further enlarged by our new relationship. In the months that followed, always meeting in the same place, when we made love as if our lives depended on it, she never once demanded anything of me in the form of promises, or that I would leave my wife, or even that there would be a next time. One day, as we lay in each other's arms and I felt the luxurious weight of her breasts against me, I said, 'I think I love you', to which she replied, 'You don't love me the way you think you do.' The Provos had again bombed London, maiming dozens and causing havoc, but we never referred to it. Warm sunshine poured in the upstairs windows, drenching us bountifully, making us feel that we'd been picked out for some sort of celestial affirmation.

She was a woman for whom pleasure arose chiefly from what was in her power to give. It wasn't better with Alison than with Sugar – it was different. I was infatuated in a way that puzzled me, since at home with my wife, when we lay sweat-soaked in the aftermath of making love, I was happy. But with Alison an additional ingredient existed. She was Alison.

A desperation began to taint the edge of our trysts, since she mentioned that there would soon be a new ambassador, and that she herself would in all likelihood be transferred. She told me this as she lay on me, warmly, softly, her large supple body flexing minutely as she sought to rouse me once more, the point of her long tongue pouncing on the tiny pools of flesh at the base of my ears. I fancied I could hear the blood rushing back to my groin. And so could she, for she began to slide down my big frame with the ease of a mermaid, her tongue circling my hard nipples, her lips wet through the forest of my stomach, her pauses innate with wisdom, until the covers were thrown back and she presented her face to me in profile as her lips worked me in unison with her fist.

As the weeks went by, her posting became the dominant issue. When, in early May, she told me that once she had read the new man into his job, she was being assigned to Washington, we hugged like two people in a cart on their way to the guillotine.

8

DUBLIN

June 1976

Alison had been busy for almost two weeks with her new ambassador, someone I was beginning to resent, since his hectic schedule had put an end to our afternoons in County Wicklow.

'What about tomorrow?' I asked her, on the phone.

'Not a chance.' She sounded breathless. 'This man must never sleep – wants me to work every evening. I'm staying in the embassy residence most nights.'

'Next week then?'

'I'm not sure. I know he has to go to London for a briefing, so maybe. I'll call you.'

I was disappointed, since it seemed like an opportunity lost and neither of us had an idea what we would do when she left for Washington. Her departure would, of course, simplify matters, but I feared for myself in her absence.

I spent the weekend in Waterloo, with Sugar and the children, took the Monday off and we barbecued by the lake. On Tuesday morning, the weather was so good that I called in sick, and returned to Dublin later in the Land Rover on my own, and sat out in the garden with Schubert turned to full volume on our new cassette deck, drinking enough to take the edge off my need. I wondered if I resumed my intelligence services to Alison, or her successor, if that would deal with my physical craving – but if I did, would Sugar not come to suspect it? Would I not smell of subterfuge all over again? The next morning, at nine-thirty, I arrived into Iveagh House, drank coffee, sat in on a routine meeting about the political aspects of proposed changes to the Common Fisheries Policy, returned to my office on the second floor, opened the windows that overlooked Iveagh Gardens with its carefree summer students, wondered briefly what it would be like to be eighteen again and answered my telephone. It was nearly eleven o'clock.

It was Bill O'Neill. 'Marty, there's been a bomb.'

Sugar drove the children and Fleming back to Dublin. That evening we huddled together, watching the nine o'clock news. My feeling was one of eerie detachment, as if this was all happening thousands of miles away to people I had never met. I couldn't speak, and even had I been able to, I don't know what I would have said. The government had declared a state of emergency.

'I'm sorry for the things I said about her,' Sugar said. 'Nothing would ever make me wish for this.' Like a man listening for the door latch, I tried to work out what she knew. 'I've spoken to Christopher,' she said. 'He's devastated. You read about it the whole time and it means nothing, then something like this happens to someone you know. All I can think of is the four of us going to the pictures together, or in Waterloo having a picnic, or out walking in Kerry. Her poor children.'

I must have looked stunned, which I was, although my mind was like a fretful dog, running to check each part of its squalid enclosure, darting to the points of possible weakness, doubling back, rechecking, caught within the confines of its shabby world. Gradually, the details became known, from the news bulletins, and from unofficial briefings. The ambassador's car, a Jaguar with an armour-plated underbody, had collected him from Dublin Airport shortly before ten that Wednesday morning, travelling in a four-vehicle convoy that was headed, with appalling irony, for the building in which I worked. It was to be the ambassador's introductory meeting with our minister, an arrangement Alison had not told me of, so I assumed it had been arranged since we had last spoken. A senior civil servant had sat up front beside the driver. The new ambassador and Alison were in the back. A back-road route had been chosen, known only to the embassy and the Gardaí. Less than two miles along this quiet country lane, a bomb of lethal force, concealed in a culvert, was triggered. The Jaguar was directly hit.

She was laid to rest two weeks later, not far from their holiday home on Caragh Lake, the place Christopher said she loved the most. He was pitiful, a man of my own age, but who could easily have passed for sixty, overweight, ruined by drink, cuckolded even if he didn't know it, unemployed and now bereaved. What would have happened, I kept asking myself, if all those years before I had not been offered a job in the Department of

External Affairs? Alison and Christopher would still have married, of course, and had children, but I would have been in Canada, peddling chicken feed to support my family and not standing in a cemetery in County Kerry, grieving more than I could ever show.

9

DUBLIN

September – November 1976

The sense of failure was enormous. Our security services were inept, our intelligence inadequate, our response to the murder of the ambassador and a good woman predictably hysterical. The fact that the Provos had been tipped off as to the route from the airport by someone inside our security services didn't bear thinking about. Thousands of Gardaí and army personnel had their leave cancelled and spent fruitless man hours in a hunt for killers they knew would never be apprehended. The emphatic assurances of the Taoiseach that those responsible would be brought to justice sounded hollow even to those who wanted to believe him. Any betting man with even half an idea of how things worked in Ireland would have had money on the outcome: no one would ever stand trial for Alison's or the ambassador's death.

I knew I had myself to blame, for if Armagh had gone to plan two years before, there was a chance this might not have happened. His handwriting was all over it. The precision of the blast, the clinical efficiency of the bomb. I spent weeks trying to come to terms with this new conflict: he had taken from me something beyond love. As if he had blown me up too. All of which, of course, was muddled, since I had always known what I was getting into and that Alison was no innocent, but had been part of a potent intelligence apparatus that threatened everything he stood for.

And me? Just a minor player with whom history had not yet adequately dealt. But soon would, I expected, even as I hoped against hope that I was wrong. I was trapped in a seething kind of phoney peace that I could discuss with no one, until, in the second week in September, at eight on a Monday evening in Sandymount, the private line in my study rang and I answered it.

'We need to talk, chum,' my caller said.

Heavy rain blurred my windscreen near the ferry port in Dún Laoghaire, so that I never saw him until the door opened.

'D'you know what I'm going to do when I retire?'
His outer coat was sodden and his hair, still showing traces of its former russetness, was plastered across his head. 'Live in bloody Spain, that's what. Or the Canaries. Or Gibraltar. Or some other bloody place where the sun shines. God, I just hate the weather in these parts, don't you?'

'Sometimes. But then there are days down in the southeast, out on the mountains, even in weather like this, when it's quite beautiful.'

'Of course, I'd forgotten you're a toff, Marty. Blue blood and all that pack-drill. You chaps never feel the cold.'

He played such a convoluted game, Vance, flattering me, or so he thought, as if life had always to be represented other than what it really was. In outline, his nose looked bigger and more curved than I had remembered, his eyelashes even longer and silkier, like feminine props to his thickset face. I assumed he had come in by ferry, but knew better than to ask him.

'How do you feel, chum?'

'Perfectly fine.'

'Because if you didn't, I would have concerns.'

'For whom?'

He laughed quietly. 'Good question. Family well?'

'Yes, thank you. Yours?'

'Tip-top actually. I'm sure it's the same over here, but the cost of education in England is scandalous. It was the same in our day, I dare say. Thirty quid a term and still my old man was always in arrears. I knew it too, which made it worse, so I used to spin the school a yarn about how he was really working in the diplomatic service and that he was abroad a lot, which was why he hadn't paid. Funny, isn't it? I ended up living in my yarn.'

He had wanted to meet a month earlier but I had put him off; I had needed time to make a rational decision. My position was made no easier by the fact that I could not allow Sugar to see the extent of my grief, or speak to her, or to anyone, of how bereft I felt for the loss of someone who had been so important to me. I pined all day, every day, for Alison. And I had become consumed by the need to respond on her behalf.

'How is her family?'

'There is of course a decent pension with benefits that will accrue to them,' Vance began, frowning.

'Otherwise ...' A squall blew in from sea and rattled the car. 'The night after it happened, the Provos partied into the small hours. For them, it was like winning the Grand National,' he said.

Feelings of loathing I had never known surged in me. 'How did they learn the route from the airport?' I asked, even though I knew the answer.

'They were tipped off by some patriot or other working in your Gardaí,' Vance said. 'Sadly, the capacity to block radio signals such as the one that triggered the bomb, hasn't reached here yet.'

Strange when the future is laid out so clearly, as it was then.

'I take it there's no doubt. I mean, about his involvement.'

'None whatsoever, chum. The ordnance was the same as he has used before. Czechoslovakian Semtex that came in here via Libya, ball-bearings, American transistors, you name it. He might as well have left a note. He's become quite the celebrity up there, you know.' Vance wiped his mouth on the back of his hand. 'Alison hated the little bugger.'

'You're absolutely sure it was him.'

'It was their south Armagh specialist. His name is Ignatius Kane.'

During MI5's post-mortem of the failed Armagh operation, two years before, someone would have, at the very least, raised the possibility that I had tipped off Iggy. Film footage may have been available. If a decision had been reached that I was the real culprit, then Vance would now regard me as expendable. On the other hand, if that was the position, would Alison not have warned me?

'A simple question, Vance.'

'By all means.'

'What if I don't want to become involved?'

'You mean...?'

'If I don't want to help you bring this to a conclusion.'

Vance's nose twitched. 'Is there any point in such a discussion?'

Rain corrugated the car's windows.

'Basically,' he said, 'one chooses one's chums for the long haul. Over the years, both sides benefit from the arrangement, even flourish from it. Give and take and all that. Intimacies are exchanged in an atmosphere of mutual trust. Each of us learns hush-hush things about the other side. Then, one day, and this always crops up, something really bad happens that leads one chum to make a big demand on the other.' From his sleeve, like a conjurer, he withdrew a green handkerchief and attended to his nose. 'Except, in our line of work, the friendship can never end, if you get my drift. Too many intimacies, too much hush-hush to let go walkabout, so to speak. We just have to keep going, best we can, as if always preparing for the next step. The defining moment really.'

I had not expected to be told anything else, but was curious, nonetheless, to hear my position laid out so starkly.

'This is very close to home,' I said. 'They may rumble me.'

'Any reasons for saying that? Beyond normal apprehension, of course?'

'Just a feeling,' I said. 'Bill O'Neill, for example.'

'Ah, Mr O'Neill.'

'He's been acting strangely.'

He had, too, ever since the Provos had come to the gates of Dublin. As he got older, Bill had become more self-preoccupied, more introverted, not just with me but with everyone in our section. He and I seldom chatted informally now, or exchanged gossip.

'We know to our cost that within your Gardaí there are officers with strong republican leanings, particularly men stationed along the border,' Vance was saying. 'It is impossible that their true allegiances are not known to some in Dublin. These officers are more than tolerated, is how I would put it. Yet your name never arises. And it would do so, were it in the general mix, so to speak. And if it were, then Mr O'Neill would be involved. But he isn't. In other words, we don't believe you have a problem.'

'What do you hear otherwise about O'Neill?'

'That not far beneath the surface is an unbendable republican.'

'And yet I'm safe?'

'Yes, we're sure of it.'

'That operation in Armagh was a stupid error,' I said, pushing it out. 'It was idiotic.'

Vance's eyebrows rose fractionally. 'By which you mean—?'

'An idiotic error by your people, Vance. Look what happened. It should never have been attempted. It was incompetent.'

I watched him closely, for surely if I had become expendable he would not be able to resist a flicker of disdain for my brazenness. Instead, he said, 'Look, this will be very different. We have a plan, of which you will be informed, when the moment comes, and although it will not be easy, it will succeed.'

'What do you mean by *succeed*? At whose expense?'

Vance sighed. 'We're not going to throw you to the wolves, Marty.'

'They will suspect me.'

'Of course, which makes you absolutely perfect for the task.'

I knew then that these people were far cleverer than I would ever be, and that by choosing them as my allies, years before, I had placed my life in a brace from which it could never escape.

'But it goes without saying that you should always be concerned,' Vance went on. 'And so, even though we would never knowingly put you in harm's way, yes, of course, we have procedures. A plan. In the event of. The plan is we get you out. That has always been a given. That's what friends are for.'

'When you say get me out...?'

'We're talking tiny percentage chances, but yes, a complete identity package in a new location for you, Sugar, the two children. Somewhere they'll never find you, and believe me, we know what we're doing. Within the UK sometimes works. So do Australia and Canada. Big countries, full of strangers moving in and out. Perfect.'

It was bizarre to think that a parallel life had been created for me and my family and that it had stood by, waiting to be used, all these years.

'So, shall we proceed?' he said.

I sighed. 'I'm going to guess how you've decided to flush him.'

Vance glanced at me and for a brief moment his expression was that of the cheeky boy I'd known twenty-five years before.

'You're going to use his sick daughter,' I said.

'My word. Quite the old operator you've become, chum.'

10

WATERFORD

December 1976

Georgie, at seven, was already turning into a gorgeous version of her mother. She was going to be taller than Sugar, with her mother's nose and fleeting expressions, her sideways glances and her little smiles that left me helpless. She and I went to eleven o'clock mass in the cathedral the Sunday before Christmas. I was a fraud in religion as I was in so many other aspects of my life: I believed in nothing, yet clung to the prayers like a character actor fitting in once again to a familiar part.

'I'm going to have a drink with Mr Gillece,' I said to Georgie as we walked back to the car. 'I'll be no more than twenty minutes.'

Unlike the previous operation, when I had baulked, this time I felt no visceral hesitation, no call from the walking dead. This time I was briefed and ready. Broad Street was strewn with litter. Outside Bobby's Bar, empty beer crates were stacked ten high. I was led by a teenage barman through the thick smoke of the pub and into the hall of the house as Bobby emerged from an understairs

207

nook he used as an office. He slammed shut the door of this tiny room and steered me to the kitchen.

'It's bad,' he said grimly. 'He was on last night, in a desperate state. The baby is too weak to operate on; she's on oxygen. They say it's terrible to watch.'

'God help them.'

'They can't even bring her home for Christmas, and, of course, he's only seen her once in the last four or five weeks; it's just too dangerous for him. Those bastards are only waiting for him to show himself.' Bobby began to pound the table with his fist until I thought he would injure himself. 'I mean, is there no decency? Even during wars in the fucking Middle Ages they allowed safe passage in these kinds of situations.'

Over his shoulder I could see the faces out at the bar, local merchants I recognised, pushing forward, as they called out their orders.

'Can she not be moved to a hospital down here?' I asked and felt a spike of unwanted hope.

'She could, but we don't have the equipment or the know-how. She's in the best hands she can possibly be in.' Irony was not something Bobby was attuned to. 'I'm going up there. To give them support.'

'A great idea.'

'I mean, we're all he has at the end of the day.' He looked at me narrowly. 'We could go up together.'

'I'm not so sure, Bobby.'

'Come on! We'd be up and down in no time!'

'You know, after our last visit . . .'

My arm was grabbed. 'Come with me. Come with me and, even though we may not meet him, the fact that we came up to see his child will mean a lot at a time like this.'

'I'd like to, Bobby, I really would, but, you know, under the circumstances, given my job and Iggy's problems—'

'All the more reason for you to come with me!' Bobby cried. 'Come on!'

I felt a vicarious pride for Vance's perspicacity. 'When had you in mind?'

'As soon as possible. The child is dying.'

'How long has she got?'

Bobby's vein-ruptured cheeks filled out into little balloons. 'From what he told me, she'll hardly see in the New Year.'

On Christmas Eve Bobby and I were both in Wise's grocery, attending to final shopping items.

'I was expecting a call from you,' I said.

Bobby coughed at length. 'They're in chaos. Iggy's in a bad way; he thinks he's not going to see the child again. I spoke to Jennifer. They're trying to see if they can arrange it so that he sees her over Christmas.'

'Are we going up?'

Bobby's little eyes blinked defensively. 'I was told not to tell anyone until the night before.'

'If I'm going, you'd better tell me,' I said.

'Stephen's Day,' Bobby said and wiped his nose. 'I've told Kate I'm going to Leopardstown races.'

Instead of driving home directly with our smoked ham, wine and a crate of tangerines, I drove to the crown of the city, to the warren of streets around Ballybricken, and parked at a corner for thirty minutes. It was dark and a fog had stolen in from the river. When I was sure I had not been followed, or observed, I got out and walked fifty yards to a public call box. I dialled the long number and pressed button A. My coins fell noisily.

'December twenty-sixth,' I said and hung up.

But on the following evening, which was Christmas Day, Auntie Kate called to say that Bobby was in bed with a temperature of a hundred and four, and that I was to go to Leopardstown races on my own.

11

Saint Stephen's Day 1976

I have often reflected during these past years, when I have had more than ample time for reflection, on what happened next.

That Saint Stephen's Day was Emmet's fourteenth birthday and we had all been invited to a lawn meet at Main, a local tradition of some importance, at which the Santrys' hospitality was once more on offer to the locality. Sugar was disappointed when I told her that I was going to the races. 'On your son's birthday?'

'I'll be back later.'

'You're not turning into the Captain, are you?' she asked.

As I set out and began to crawl northwards on an icy road, the towns and villages I passed through seemed deserted, or dead. In County Kildare, drenched horses stood with hindquarters to the wind in slanting drizzle. There were several occasions when I almost lost my nerve. At traffic lights in Dublin, I may even have made the decision to turn around, but then the lights went green and I drove on. What did I owe to Vance and his like compared to the fond memories of my childhood that would always endure for me? I didn't have to do this, I kept telling myself. I could easily have telephoned a number and called off the operation that was already in motion. My day could indeed have been spent at the races; I could have been the Captain for the afternoon; I would still have been home in time for Emmet's birthday party. In those dreamy moments when we all fantasise about living our lives again, of going back in time with the advantage of foreknowledge, I have asked myself a hundred times what I would have done differently that day, and I have always come to the same conclusion. Nothing. Bring me back in time, I say to the God I once believed in, bring me back and I would do it all over again.

Snow lay in thin ridges in the car park. I counted six other cars and a boxy blue Ford van, all of them with Northern Ireland registrations. The noon-day Angelus was ringing out over Newry as I hurried into the hospital.

Christmas decorations were everywhere in the empty lobby. Behind a raised reception counter a man was reading a book. When I coughed, he looked up. His bald head was startlingly white and elliptical.

'The hospital is closed.'

'The door was open.'

'It's Christmas. Everyone's been sent home; there's no one here.'

'I've come to visit a sick child. Jenny Kane. I've come a long way.'

Large, round eyes bestowed his face with qualities of childlike innocence. He put down his book.

'We're officially closed,' he said, picking up a phone. 'Who shall I tell them?'

'Uncle Marty.'

He dialled, spoke quietly, replaced the receiver. 'If you'd like to take a seat.'

Low-slung, tweed-upholstered armchairs with wooden arms overlooked the car park. In Leopardstown, they would be drinking hot toddies. Where had the old days gone, when nothing more than a betting coup was at stake? I heard lift doors trundling open and then a young man with a flaming beard was walking towards me. His dark polo neck and anorak were somehow instantly sinister.

'I'm Ted Junior, Uncle Marty. Remember me?'

A packet of Marlboros appeared in his hands as he sat and we both lit up. 'You've come alone.'

'Bobby sends his best wishes, but unfortunately—'

'I know, Kate called. It's bad luck on him over Christmas and all. But you're well, Uncle Marty?'

'We're all feeling for you. How is little Jenny?'

'Baby Jenny's dying. She's been anointed twice, the last time just this morning. She's going straight to heaven.'

'Of course.'

'She's an example to all of us. She gives us the strength to go on. She makes us brave.'

He was not quite as tall as me, but he was broad in the shoulders. When he spoke, he had a way of smiling briefly, and it took me a few moments to work it out: he was the image of Uncle Ted, my uncle.

'How are her parents?'

'Jennifer's here, of course, she's not left little Jenny's bedside for a month. Iggy's the problem.' His smile

213

beamed for an instant from his beard. 'He can't risk coming here to see his little girl. It's the reality. We understand the reality. We created it.'

'I wish there was something I could do.'

'Your being here means a lot. A lot to Iggy.'

'I can only try to imagine how he feels.'

'Angry at the beginning, but better now. We talk to him every night, bring him Polaroids, he sends her in his carved wooden animals.'

'That's lovely.'

He ground out his cigarette. 'Would you like to see her?'

'I don't want to intrude.'

'You're part of our family, Uncle Marty.'

'I'll just come in very briefly,' I said as a man suddenly appeared, his dark hair sprinkled with snow.

'Could you just let us have the keys to your car for a moment, Uncle Marty?'

'My car?'

'Just for a wee minute, if that's all right with you. We need to move it for you.'

The man who had come in was looking at me from enlarged orbs, as if I were a species that up to now he had only heard of. I handed him my keys.

'We'd better go up,' Ted said. 'They'll be wondering what happened to me.'

The heat was excessive and I unbuttoned my coat as we stepped into the lift. As we ascended, the building seemed to hum all around us. A life-size statue of the Virgin Mary with a halo made of tiny electric lights appeared on the third floor when the lift doors opened and was bizarrely comforting. Was there anything in my car – anything at all – that could give them what I now knew they were looking for? The empty wards were still jarringly cheerful with their streamers and Santa Clauses. Ted Junior held open the door to a room beside a fire escape.

'After you, Uncle Marty.'

Death, as it approaches, sends out an almost tangible atmosphere, not quite a vapour, not quite a smell, more like a soupy kinetic field of inevitability. I had experienced it in Kenya, when I had escaped it, and, as a child, in the Gent's abattoir, where terrified sheep and pigs awaited their fate.

A waxen infant lay in bed beside a machine with a greenly winking panel. Jennifer, Iggy's wife, sat, holding the child's hand. Patrick, Ted Junior's twin brother, was standing beside the door to a bathroom and stared at me as I came in. Jennifer was brushing the child's hair.

'I'm sorry it has to be like this,' I whispered to her.

'We all must live our lives, however short they may be,' she said.

'I'm sorry Iggy can't be here.'

She looked at me with mild curiosity, then smiled sadly.

'Uncle Marty?' Ted Junior swivelled his head towards the bathroom. 'A word in private?'

At such moments, my life compresses into tiny fractions of time. I wondered if I should try to take one of them with me, and what exactly Sugar was doing then, or if the hunt at Main had moved off. I'm a big man, but as I stepped in to the bathroom, I was shoved violently from behind and pitched forward onto the tiled floor.

'What…?'

Ted Junior was standing over me, pointing a pistol in my face.

'Take all your fuckin' clothes off, Uncle Marty. Take them off now!'

'What?'

'Take your fuckin' clothes off!' His gun hand was steady. 'Every stitch.'

Trembling, I got up and began to undress. 'You're making a big mistake.'

'Then explain the day of the ordination, Marty.' Patrick was standing behind me. 'Explain how you knew. You can't, can you? Because then you'd have to tell us who you really are.'

He'd backed away and was minutely examining each article of clothing as I removed it, turning out my pockets. With a carpet cutter, he began to reef the collar and lining of my jacket, shredding the garment and spilling out its wadding.

'The ordination, Marty.' Ted Junior poked the cold barrel into my ear. 'Tell us real quick about the day of the ordination!'

'I ... I saw a helicopter,' I said as I stepped from my underpants, 'and suddenly realised what was going to happen.'

'Kneel in the shower and face the wall.'

'Iggy and I had an old code from when we were children.'

Ted Junior clubbed me across the neck with the handle of the gun.

'Kneel down in the shower and face the fuckin' wall!'

As my knees hit cold tiles, I thought of the one person I had so loved but who had also died violently. A knife blade clicked and I braced. From the corner of my eye, I could see Patrick slicing my overcoat to pieces.

'What are you looking for?'

'You know what I'm fuckin' looking for and you know if we find it here or in your car, you're a dead man,' Patrick said.

I made myself laugh. 'You think I'm working for the Brits? That I've come here with some sort of a transmitting device? You're out of your minds. You've completely misjudged the situation.'

'Just shoot the cunt,' Patrick said. 'Put him out of his misery.'

'You won't find anything in my clothes because there isn't anything to find, and there isn't because I'm not who you think I am.'

'Stand up! Hands on the wall! Spread your legs! Now!'

I stood in an outstretched position, and then gasped as I felt the crude, blunt force of a finger in a rubber glove ram upwards into my rectum.

'Christ!'

'Now you know what it feels like.' I heard Patrick snap the glove off. 'We'll give you one last chance. Tell us who you're working for, who you report to, what you know about Iggy, what plans the Brits have for Iggy, and we won't kill you.'

My shivering was beyond my control. 'You know exactly who I am and for whom I work. I speak with an English accent because that is how my parents spoke and because I was sent to school in England.'

He pressed the gun into the back of my neck and my legs went from under me.

'Last chance, Marty.'

From where I curled, I said, 'Of course we exchange

217

information with the Brits. Of course we use them to try to keep abreast of what's going on up here.' He clicked off the safety and I peed warmly down my thighs. 'So, yes, I did hear, but not in any way that I could confirm, that there might be some trouble following the ordination mass – which is why I went to Armagh in the first place. To warn Iggy. Which I did. Do you know how close he and I are? We're like brothers. All I would ever want to do is protect him. I love Iggy Kane and up to five minutes ago I thought that he loved me.'

Someone knocked on the bathroom door and I could hear the sound of keys. Ted Junior's gun was inserted into my ear again. 'You're full of shit Marty! You could just as easily have made a call. Or told Bobby Gillece so that he could have warned us.'

'Bobby? A man who hasn't been sober for twenty-five years? Or send a message by telephone? I don't know much, but this much I do know: there's a war going on and, in a war, you trust no one but those close to you.'

'That's the world we operate in,' Ted Junior said. 'Twenty-four-hour surveillance, eyes in the sky, tracking devices put into our cars. So we trust no one, not even those close to us. But because you're close to us, we're giving you this one last chance.'

'I can't tell you what I don't know.'

'Do you not know why you were screwing that fat bitch?' Patrick shouted in my ear. 'Mrs Alison Chase? You're one of them, Marty! Admit it now!' I began to weep, but not for myself. 'Do it!' Patrick said urgently. 'Do it quick!'

There was silence. I grasped myself and waited for the blankness. *Just like turning out a light.*

My underclothes landed on the floor outside the shower.

'You can get up, Uncle Marty,' Ted Junior said. 'I'm sorry. We had to be sure.'

I made it to my feet, but then my knees gave way again and the two lads caught me.

12

NEWRY, COUNTY ARMAGH

Saint Stephen's Day 1976

Except for the voice of the bald-headed receptionist, on the telephone in his back office, all was quiet in the hospital lobby. Upstairs they'd replaced my clothes with a kind of boiler suit and given me a woollen jacket. After I had puked at length, they had turned on the shower and made sure that I was clean before I dressed.

Patrick Kane suddenly appeared in the lobby, walking briskly. He went outside, ran to a black Austin Cambridge parked there, started it up and drove to the hospital doors. Engine exhaust rose in a thick white tail, whiter than the day. I heard the lift again and then Jennifer appeared, carrying her infant well wrapped up in both arms. On one side of her walked a priest, on the other a nurse wearing an outer coat over her white uniform. Patrick was holding open the door to the hospital. In less than a minute they had driven away. Then, as I watched, the blue Ford van pulled out and drove from the car park at a leisurely pace. The receptionist had not even bothered to come out and observe the departure of his hospital's solitary patient.

'Uncle Marty?' Ted Junior must have been standing behind me all along. 'You all right?'

'I'm fine, thank you, yes,' I said. 'But I think I'll go home now. D' you have my keys?'

'They're upstairs. Come up with me and we'll get them.'

Unhurriedly, we went to the lift. On the third floor, as the doors opened to the halo of lights, he broke into a run. 'Come on!'

By the time I had caught up and reached the bedroom he had already scooped up the baby. 'The fire escape! Go!' Two bars stood out from the doors at waist height. 'Kick them!'

I expected an alarm, but the whistle of wind was the only sound as I zigzagged down to the foot of the metal structure where my car was parked.

'Uncle Marty.' He lobbed the keys at me. 'You're driving.'

The infant's chest rose in laboured gasps. I followed his instruction into a maze of stark housing and ten minutes later began to recognise some of the landmarks – a school, a burned-out car. We were driving in circles.

'It's having to do what we're doing at this minute that turns ordinary men into soldiers. One day they're going to remember the name of little Jenny Kane, aren't they Jenny? Aye? That's a great girl.'

With the heater turned to high, we left the town as daylight began to ebb. Trees stood out bleakly. The baby shuddered. Little frozen hills gave way to glens swaddled in evening mist. It was really quite beautiful. I pulled in, as Ted told me to, under a tree canopy and switched off the engine. He wound down his window and listened. I could hear nothing, except for the baby as she battled to breathe.

'And, of course, if you are one of them, Uncle Marty, they'll hardly take us out, now, will they?' Ted Junior chuckled as we drove on again. 'Not if you're one of their own.'

I was now certain that Vance's plan, whatever that was, had been outsmarted. My ordeal in the bathroom had left me drained to a point where I could wonder what was going to happen next with a detachment bordering on indifference. I wondered where Iggy would be waiting. I would mean nothing to him in this context: just a man with a clean car. I was irrelevant to Iggy, and that marked the difference between us: he was not to me.

The road followed the crests of little rises, then plunged into valleys of dead ferns etched in white fronds as precise as filigree. We turned down an unpaved road with sunken wheel ruts and the underside of my car scraped earth. The infant panted and gasped. Ahead towered the deep black wall of a coniferous forest.

'Pull up and turn off the engine.'

Within thirty seconds the cold had begun to seep in. Lights flashed. A Toyota jeep drew across our track and two men jumped from it, both in standard army camouflage and woollen head masks. One stood at the front of the car, pointing an AKM assault rifle at me; the other went to Ted Junior's side.

'You weren't followed?'

'Definitely not.'

'How's the wee bairn?'

Ted Junior bent to the baby's head and kissed her.

'What about him?'

'He's clean,' Ted Junior said. 'Patrick and me checked him. And the car.'

The man came around to my window. 'Is the boot locked?'

'I don't believe so.'

As the boot was opened and I heard him rummaging, the gunman never lowered his aim. His companion now went to the jeep and took out a long metal pole that ended in a dish-like mirror. He began to inspect the car's underbody.

'Ted!'

One of the gunmen was listening intently. Through the trees, as if through a giant lung, came the soughing wind. We were all straining, but the quality of silence beyond the wind was gapingly empty. The man with the inspection mirror came to my window.

'Follow us. Stay glued. Don't even think of turning your lights on.'

The jeep swung around and I drove into the forest within five yards of its tow-hitch. Daylight died.

'She's never going to come out of here,' Ted Junior said. 'The only blessing is she knows nothing.'

A dull fatalism had taken me over, in which all fear was absent and my concerns for my own safety evaporated. I no longer cared. My career had amounted in the end to nothing more than this dark, dead place. All at once the jeep stopped.

'Come on, love.' Ted Junior opened the door.

Maybe a hundred years before, when the lee side of this mountain had been a bare, treeless place, a man had built his cottage here. All that remained were two walls, including the curved granite lintel of the front door, gracefully intact. Ted Junior gathered the infant close, although the cold within this forest was less piercing. Iggy walked out from the ruined house.

'Hello, Iggy.'

He strafed me with a look, then he went to his child.

'You'd best sit her in the car,' Ted Junior was saying as Iggy took his daughter and kissed her. Even in the dim light I could see that his hair was grey.

'You can't take these nails out, Marty. These ones are driven right through my heart.'

'*Iggy!*'

A man from the jeep had begun to shout.

'Oh, Jesus, no!' Ted Junior cried.

And then our little group was pinned in blinding light as noise made further communication impossible. Ted Junior put his arm around his half-brother's slight shoulders, but Iggy's jaw was set as he clutched his child. The gunmen were firing at the sky as the trees seemed to bend inwards. Dropping from the car, I rolled into cold, crisp ferns. Any minute I expected the impact. I hit a tree, flung myself around it and kept rolling. My back hurt. I think I heard automatic weapons discharging but I could not be sure since the racket was so intense. After more than a minute I got up and ran. Every few hundred yards, I stopped and listened. It didn't take long for the natural silence to be restored.

When I left the forest, the night was clear and bright and the skinned land stood out starkly. Downhill, through tiny fields, by a stone wall, I removed Ted Junior's jacket and put my lighter to it. I felt the glow as the cheap fabric caught the flame. A few minutes later I ground the ashes with my heel and covered what remained with stones.

I used the evening star as my waypoint. The same star hung over our mountain on a good night and had never let me down. The cold didn't bother me and my step lightened, despite an insistent ache in my back. Most of my life was still ahead of me and I had much to be thankful for.

Part IV

Part IV

GUELPH LINE, CAMPBELLVILLE, ONTARIO

The Recent Past

Sometimes she sees them as figures in a canvas, as if there has been a mistake and they have somehow entered another dimension. At such moments, she becomes convinced that the present is provisional and that time is simply being marked here while a more suitable space is being prepared, into which they will shortly move, a fresh plane where the past will be regained quite naturally.

Maria Fernanda's Saturdays come around so quickly now that it is impossible to believe another week has gone by since the intercom last signalled her arrival. When they sit down with her for tea – an initiative that he was not at first disposed towards – and Maria Fernanda tells them of the señor's recent health setbacks, in the days that follow she finds herself hoping that a man she has never met will pass away, in the shameful belief that they will then have more of Maria Fernanda to themselves.

She has not seen Emmet in many years. He too changed his name and, from what she can gather, lives somewhere in Europe. He is married to a French woman and they have grown-up children whom she will never meet. It seems like only a few weeks ago that she had wrapped him up against the snow on the day of the point-to-point. She never blamed him for wanting to begin again, on his own. Despite everything, against all the odds, she believes in hope and in the mercy of Providence.

1

PARIS

1979

Ireland steadily expanded her embassies during the 1970s, providing openings for rank-and-filers like me who wanted to see a bit of the world. In the second half of 1977 I was posted with the position of secretary to Greece, and in 1979 to Paris, where one morning, sitting outside Fouquet's with a *grand crème*, and reading the *Daily Telegraph*, I sat back with a shock as the photograph of a man jumped out at me from the obituaries page. His career in the Foreign Office had been distinguished, the paper said, and he had contributed to a number of important intergovernmental protocols, particularly involving the United Kingdom and Ireland. His death followed a short illness, it said. He was survived by his wife and two sons. I read and re-read the obituary. He had never made it to the South of France, but what surprised me most, I think, was that his first name was Reginald.

2

Dublin Airport

May 1977

Tired-looking airline crews stood around the hotel reception waiting to be allocated rooms. By the lifts, ugly rubber plants spilled from ceramic pots. Five floors up, I knocked on a door. He was sniffling and still wore his raincoat. The bed in the poky room had not been slept in. Outside, midday sun spanked from the windscreens of airport traffic.

'I'm glad you haven't caught this, chum, although now you probably will. But perhaps not. You upper-class types have a far superior immune system to us commoners. It's true! You're tough old buggers.'

He poured boiling water into two glasses, added honey from tiny plastic containers, took out a naggin of John Jameson's from the pocket of his raincoat and decanted it generously.

'Cheers, old boy. How is Sugar? The children? And of course, how are you?'

'We're all very well, thanks.'

'That's the main thing, isn't it? Your health. I mean, money is important, but health is everything.'

'Apart from your working-class cold, are you well, Vance?'

He laughed somewhat bitterly. 'I sometimes wonder if I'll ever get my head above water. When I started out, I had this dream that before I reached forty, I would have it made. Well up the ladder, mortgage paid off, a second house somewhere in the sun, my boys in private schools. I always thought my father was a failure – bloody articled clerk all his life. He and my mother hated each other, drank too much, never took a continental holiday. I'll be forty this year and I suddenly understand all the shit he put up with just to send me to a good school.' He closed his eyes for a moment, and then drank his whiskey in two gulps. 'Ah! That's better! So, how's the job, chum?'

There was a greyness to his pallor that I had not noticed before.

'Place is being reorganised. We are opening new embassies, so there are opportunities. Nothing concrete yet, but I've applied.'

'Ah, how I envy you! The ex-pat life, aye? Servants, duty-free booze, never have to pay a parking ticket. Some place in Africa would be perfect for me. Big game, good climate, a swimming pool. The empire, you see! It may be on the way out but it still has its uses.' He was checking his wristwatch. 'Now, I must be on a flight, so alas can't hang about and chat, much as I'd like to. Just to say, much appreciated and all that pack-drill. Job well done.'

'I'm glad you're pleased,' I said cautiously.

'You did a brave and honourable thing, chum, not that

I would ever have doubted it, mind you, but you can be proud. Society is a better place.'

'For me it was personal.'

'Ah, yes, yes.' For a moment, he was caught in a private reflection, but quickly shook himself out of it. 'Chum, you and I probably won't be seeing much of each other from now on. Always a matter of regret, but there you go, part of our trade, I suppose. By the way, from our point of view, from what we can hear up there, there's no noise, if you get my meaning.'

'You mean, about me. You mean up in the North?'

'Absolutely nothing. Zero. You're clear. Just carry on is my advice.'

'They don't forget or forgive easily up there. Or down here.'

'If they held you responsible, we would know about it. One hundred thousand per cent guaranteed. But they don't. You're clear.'

'How exactly did you track us into the forest?'

'Your car, chum. We bugged your car.'

I gaped. 'Shit, Vance! You did what?'

'Bugged it. Fitted a tracking device.'

'But they checked my car.'

'Well, they thought it had been checked, chum. Yes, that's what they thought.'

'I could easily have been killed.'

'Indeed, but of course it was never our intention to put you in harm's way. If we had known they were going to bring you with them, as they did, and expose you to danger, we would never have gone ahead with the plan. We reckoned they would just take your car, but we never imagined they would take you as well.'

I had to admire them, even then. A man whose dark hair was sprinkled with snow. Taking my keys. Staring at me from enlarged orbs as if I was a species he had up to then just heard of. And my car must have been fitted out, without my knowing it, before I ever left the south-east.

'Look,' Vance was saying, 'he was a low-level little shit. Lethal, of course, but still low-level. They'll replace him, we know, but the message was the important thing. We delivered the message. It's over.'

'Then why are you here, Vance?'

He looked at me curiously. 'To say goodbye, old boy. We're not machines, you know.' He shook his head, as if he might have been offended. 'And to tie up some loose ends.'

I felt my heart skip. 'Go on.'

He rearranged his legs, and shifted in the chair as if his impending statement required a different position.

'You once asked me to do something,' he said in a voice that was suddenly conciliatory. 'To make certain enquiries.'

'Yes, I did.'

'About Captain Ransom.'

'Yes.'

He winced and joined his hands, then splayed them out towards me, palms first, in a series of clicks. 'Well, you see, the reason why your old man was never cremated, and a death certificate never issued, is that he was never found.'

I stood up. 'How do you mean, "never found"? He died of a heart attack in Green Park.'

Vance looked pained. 'On the evening of Saturday, 24th January 1953, a man was killed in a fight outside the

Victoria Stakes, a pub near Alexandra Park Racecourse in Haringey, North London. Although no witnesses came forward, and no one was ever charged, police at the time said they wished to question a Patrick Kane, also known as Paddy Ransom, whose address was The Prince's Arms public house, Hammersmith.'

'Who was the dead man?'

'A well-known con artist named Frederick Black, a man with convictions for embezzlement.'

'Mr Black!'

'Frederick Black, yes.'

'I always knew he was a crook. So did my mother. Why did they fight?'

'Apparently Black owed your old man money. But that aside, two days later, clothing belonging to Patrick Kane was found beside the Thames in Battersea,' Vance said grimly.

'Oh, God.'

'I'm afraid so, old boy.'

'His greatcoat, shoes, hat and wallet,' I said.

'Exactly. You see, he must have drowned, poor chap, then been washed out to sea.'

I don't know why, because he'd been dead for nearly a quarter of a century, but I was seized by grief. 'So he's not alive,' I heard myself say.

Vance flinched. 'No, I'm afraid not. I have of course been in touch with the police, on and off, on your behalf – they've kept an eye out for years. Places like Tangiers, but there's never been a sighting. Sorry, chum.'

I was deflated to a point that I knew was not reasonable, not after so long, but nonetheless that is how I felt.

'He was a wonderful chap, your old man, no doubt

whatsoever that is what he was, and that is how you should remember him, old boy. A really first-class man.'

Through the weight of my sorrow, something about Vance's words, the way he had just delivered them, riveted me. I straightened up. 'How long have you known this?'

'How long? Let me see – it took quite a lot of winkling to get the files from Scotland Yard.'

'When did you first know that my father had in all likelihood committed suicide? When?'

Vance bit his lip and, for perhaps the first time ever, I saw guilt in his big, broad face.

'I want to know, Vance.'

'Look,' he said, 'all right, chum, but it was all done to protect your feelings.'

'My God.'

He sighed. 'I was head prefect. Nessie was terrified. Your mother had telephoned him constantly for over a week when they'd been searching for your old man. "Under no circumstances is this boy to be told his father may have drowned himself, do you understand?" was what Nessie told me. Of course, if the old fool hadn't said that, I'd not have had the slightest idea, but he was so confused, he said it.'

'You've always known!'

'Steady on ...'

I had him by the throat, and slammed him against the door of the cheap, sliding wardrobe. His face bulged like a rubber ball.

'You've always fucking known! All these years!'

He was gurgling and I suddenly realised that I wanted nothing more than to kill him, and that if I did so, here in this anonymous shithole beside the airport, no one would ever know.

'Did Alison know? If you lie to me, I will kill you, so help me God!'

He managed to shake his head. 'She…never did.'

Through the mist of my grief and rage, I become conscious, albeit faintly, that, despite everything, he and I were still on the same side. I let him go and he flopped down on the bed.

'I'm sorry, chum,' he heaved, 'but I did make enquiries, I really did, and the fact is that his body was never found, which is why there never was a death cert, so he could have turned up, couldn't he?'

He was rubbing his neck as I brought him a glass of water.

'I had this childish hope,' I said.

'I know you did.' He drank the water. Shakily he picked up his whiskey glass again, upended it and swallowed the golden dregs.

'Are you all right, Vance?'

'Oh, I probably deserved it. I've dreaded telling you this for years.' He shook his head. 'But it wasn't as if I could have done anything to bring him back. Look, enough of me. Now all that remains is to give you your insurance policy.'

I looked at him blankly. 'Do I need one?'

'The question I ask myself every time I write a cheque to those bloodsuckers who cover my house, my car, my holiday perils. Dear God, why did you not make a world where we don't need insurance?' He drank water again. 'In the unlikely event, as I have mentioned before, you call this number.' He handed me a white card with a phone number scribbled on it. 'This chap will sort it out. It's what he does. Of course, in the meantime, if we hear anything...'

'How unlikely, Vance?'

'Ah, Marty, you know much more about chance than I do – you're a racing man.'

With an unexpected prong of regret, I realised that we would never meet again. He moved towards the door and paused. His face was ashen but bruises were rising on his neck. 'She was wonderful, wasn't she?' he said.

'Wonderful,' I said.

'Goodbye, chum.'

3

PARIS

Spring 1981

From Saint-Cloud, I set out for work every day by train. Emmet, at nineteen, was enrolled in a nearby lyceé. Georgie's school involved a bus journey which she undertook with Nurse Fleming. I worked as a secretary, with the rank of higher executive officer, and reported to the cultural attaché from my office in our magnificent embassy on Avenue Foch. Part of my job was to help promote readings, recitals and film premieres that reflected the cultural harmony that existed between France and Ireland.

In Paris, I came to know my children as people rather than props to be tidied away. In Emmet's case, it was probably too late: he had grown up quickly in every sense and had been old enough when his mother and I had separated for those few months to understand what was happening. He may even have preferred Sugar's businessman to me. Now he smoked cigarettes and spent most of every day at the home of his French girlfriend – someone he had met at school and to whom only Sugar had been introduced. 'She's very pretty, very charming,' I was told and that made me happy for my son.

When we did meet, he displayed a healthy disdain for the way I spoke, and proclaimed my stories of the Captain, whenever recited, as ridiculous, and declared that when he was old enough to be able to do so, he was going to change his name to Kane. Nonetheless, I tried to chivvy along our relationship, taking him racing at Saint-Cloud, where he sat bored for the afternoon, and out to lunch at the better restaurants. Emmet was always polite to me, but somewhere in that murky decade where I had split myself in an effort to find my elusive soul, I had lost him.

With Georgie, it was different. She'd been just a little girl during our separation, and was ten years old when I was posted to Paris. She soon spoke French fluently and was the image of her mother; I could sometimes imagine them as two sisters as they sat at a café table or strolled on a leafy boulevard. Georgie had grown up with the post-Alison version of me. She was charming, and smiled when she saw me, and made a fuss of me, as if I were too fragile to be left to my own devices. She played tennis in Saint-Cloud, but despite inheriting her mother's talent, refused to take it seriously. Sugar was at first irked by this lack of ambition, but Georgie would have none of it. She and I rode out together from stables in the Forêt de Versailles. I knew she would make a good choice in men when the time came, a conviction that filled me with happiness.

Often, during those years of strolling by the Seine, or through the sun-dappled colonnades of the Rue de Rivoli, I thought of Alison. I kept her like an icon, for I knew she had fulfilled me in a way that no one else could have. That might have been a poor reflection on my character, but whenever I tried to imagine my life without her, I could not. She had made me feel good about myself, and had allowed me to realise my potential, however warped, and for that small miracle I was grateful. I longed for her, even when I was happy with my family, and I longed to know, which I never would, what she would have thought of what I had done. How I had deceived, then vindicated her. I liked to believe that, on balance, she would have been proud of me.

At such moments, Iggy was never very far away. I saw him in all the different ways that children perceive one another, his moods and little tricks to get attention, how he was always observing me observing him, how he charmed his dad. His indifference to punishment. The way he had treated Uncle Stanley and, finally, had dispatched the poor man. Iggy had been a strange combination of love and cruelty, a mixture he had kept to the end.

Five people had died that day in the south Armagh woodlands: Iggy, his half-brother Patrick, baby Jenny and two other members of the Provos. They had been intercepted with bomb-making equipment by the British SAS and had died resisting arrest, the official communiqué stated. Ted Kane Junior would never walk again.

The ambush made front-page news, but nowhere was I mentioned. Nor did I see my car again: I imagine it had made its way to a breakers yard somewhere in Belfast, courtesy of British Special Forces. When I got home at daybreak, having thumbed a lift to Dublin and then celebrated my escape by taking a taxi, I told Sugar that someone had rear-ended me on my way out of

Leopardstown and that my car was a write-off. It was she who insisted on examining the small of my back, where a livid bruise was flowering, and made me get into the Land Rover and drove me to Waterford where an X-ray revealed a lump of glass the size of a thumbnail embedded near my spine. A piece of my car's rear window, everyone agreed. I was operated on next morning, but the infection had already taken hold. I would not be going home for two weeks.

My first visitor, apart from my family, was Bobby Gillece. Ashen, the knuckles on his fist bulging, he stared at me.

'Did you see this?' He pointed to his newspaper and began to cry. 'Iggy is dead.'

I gasped as a wave of pain gripped me.

'What happened?' Bobby asked.

His mouth was open as I told him.

'How did you escape?' he asked eventually.

'I hit the ground and rolled.'

Bobby was blinking rapidly. 'You rolled?'

'Then I ran.'

'And does anyone—? Did anyone arrest you? Or question you?'

'No.'

'Jesus.' I saw admiration briefly capture his cat-like face. 'I mean, if I'd gone up there with you, I would most probably have been killed, too.'

A nurse came in and checked my intravenous drip.

'Only Jennifer and Ted Junior know I was up there and they're hardly likely to tell the RUC,' I said. 'By the way, you do realise that as far as Sugar is concerned, I was in a car accident in Leopardstown.'

Bobby's moustache twitched. 'What do you take me for?'

We chatted for a while about the old days, and our memories of Fowler Street, and how Granny Kane had at least been spared this tragedy. Bobby told me he was going north for the funerals.

'Please send my condolences,' I said.

'I loved him, you know,' Bobby said, and began to cry again, 'I loved him like a son.'

Iggy's obituary appeared in the local papers. WATER-FORD NATIVE DIES IN AMBUSH. It was less about Iggy than about the Kane family and their long associa-tion with the city. 'A first cousin of Mr Kane is Mr Martin Ransom, son of the late Captain Ransom, Waterloo Farm,' the obituary read, 'who works as a high-ranking official in the Department of Foreign Affairs in Dublin.'

Several national newspapers picked up the story and one of them printed my photograph, taken at least ten years earlier at a race meeting. I wondered, when I saw it, if Bill O'Neill would, at a minimum, want a chat. He never did.

Neither did Sugar, who must surely have read the papers, bring the matter up, as if over the years she had been taught the subjects to avoid. Not so with Emmet. Our son, who began every discussion from a starting point of scepticism, for which I could hardly blame him, asked, 'Are you really related to this man Ignatius Kane, like the papers say you are?'

Emmet was preparing for his Intermediate Certificate exam in the Dublin school he then attended. He was standing at the door to the kitchen, holding a textbook.

'His father and my father were brothers. And, yes, that makes us first cousins.'

'Jesus!'

'Emmet!' Sugar said.

'He was a terrorist! His whole family are terrorists. Ignatius Kane was one of the most wanted men in Ireland. And he's your cousin? He's my second cousin?'

'We cannot help being related to people,' Sugar said. 'It's outside of our control.'

'You're not related to him, Mum. I am. My friends know about this. It's so embarrassing. What do I tell them?'

I could have answered, at length, had I been so inclined, or if he had bothered to listen. I could have told him that Ireland is a very young democracy, as democracies go, and that as we work through our differences, sometimes paths diverge, even in families. In such cases, I could have gone on, even the closest childhood friends and blood relations can find themselves on opposite sides, and new alignments take shape, and we come to love differently than we did as children. I could never tell him that I loved someone so much that when she was taken from me, I drew a line through everything I had held dear before and that I would have pulled the trigger myself to put Iggy down if that had been necessary.

'Dad? What do I tell them?'

'Tell them that Ignatius Kane was nothing to us,' I said. 'Nothing at all.'

4

WATERFORD

August 1981

I returned for an unscheduled weekend, to visit my step-father, Michael, who lived alone, and who now farmed my land. Waterloo had become just a holiday home for us, albeit a highly uncomfortable one. And yet I could still taste the magic of the place as I advanced along the hip of the mountain, the feeling that up here all would be well.

The next afternoon I drove to Waterford and walked into Bobby's Bar. The local tailor, a deaf mute with curling eyebrows, who drank there in the afternoons, was the only customer. Bobby and I had lost touch, and although five years had gone by since Iggy's death, I had felt it safer to keep my distance. Even so, I had not been able to resist dropping by to test the temperature.

'Hello, Bobby.'

He was arranging bottles behind the counter and turned. For half a second – and that's all it was – he saw me with open detestation, an expression of pure abhorrence. But Bobby was a pro, and quickly broke into a smile and bellowed my name. We drank whiskey and he settled into his prattle, which had not changed, nor did he waver in his affability for the next hour, despite my pushing him to the limits of his patience. It had only been for half a second, but half a second is all you need, as the Captain had said: half a second is all a sniper is given to reorder the world to his own liking, so why should you have more?

Later that day, somewhat light-headed, I walked up to Fowler Street. So much had changed. Granny Kane had died at Sunday mass in the cathedral, an occurrence widely viewed as proof of divine involvement. Father O'Dea had just served her communion, in her pew, and she had expired, there and then, the intact host still in her mouth. (Apparently, this had caused consternation among those trying to revive her: whether or not to touch the body of Christ in order to revive the body of an elderly lady.) A decade later, the Gent and Aunt Angela had died within a month of each other and the terraced house that had been so central to my growing-up had been sold. The intricate internal details of 8 Fowler Street – its small rooms, dado rails, wallpaper, cutlery, coal scuttle, holy pictures, cotton sheets, night lights and the stair carpet that my aunts had made over three years – were engraved on the plate of my mind. As I turned into Fowler Street, I cocked my ear, for my imagination still expected the voices of the dead to welcome me.

The door was ajar. In the once tidy hallway stood half

a dozen bags of cement, piled one on the other. The staircase was missing. Stepping in, I looked up and saw that the little house had been entirely hollowed out. My first thought was: what will Iggy think of this?

5

PARIS

February 1982

We spent hours trying to work out why we were so happy.

'I saw a poster for a piano bar somewhere near here,' I said. 'They specialise in the songs of Noël Coward.'

'Mad dogs and Englishmen,' Sugar said.

We were sitting in the window booth of a bistro we greatly approved of, just off the Rue Francois 1er. Sugar had come into town from Saint-Cloud and we'd gone to the pictures. She had to peer over the platter of *fruits de mer* in order to see me.

'They should create the post of romantic attaché for you,' she said. 'The ambassador of the never-ending love affair.'

'Over here, I can give them my version of an Irishman and nobody raises an eyebrow. I can love my country without being irritated by it. I'm without issues here. I could happily do this for ever, dropping back to Waterloo for holidays. This is me.'

She used a tool like a knitting needle to extract the meat from a periwinkle.

'Then that's exactly what we should do.'

'What?'

'Come and live here.'

'I'll be posted somewhere else,' I said. 'I'm only forty-one.'

'But we should buy now so that we can come back here when you retire. I read an article in *Le Monde* that described how property in Paris is going to soar in value beyond what anyone can now imagine.'

'What about the small question of money?'

'We can use what my parents left me and raise a loan on Waterloo.'

'Your parents left you that money, not me. They wanted you to be independent, or at least your mother did.'

Sugar sat back. 'I'm serious. We've got everything we want here. I don't want to grow old in Ireland.'

I never imagined her growing old anywhere, for to me she was still the beautiful girl I had met in Main and fallen in love with.

'I'll think about it,' I said.

'We always end up talking about Waterloo – but the last twice we stayed there was when we buried our respective mothers. Do we need it, other than as a place to lodge when we attend a funeral?'

'I said I'll think about it.'

She looked curiously at me. 'It's really got quite a hold on you, hasn't it?'

'What?'

'The whole destiny thing, the idea that you're just one in a line, that your mother's family came there a hundred and fifty years ago or whatever and that it's now your responsibility, blah, blah, blah. And I can understand that. I'm just the daughter of a country rector who never possessed more than his stipend. You're different.'

'You're out of your mind,' I said. 'To hell with Waterloo. If you want to live here, this is where we'll live. We'll go to Ireland for Easter and I'll put things in motion.'

6

Paris

March 1982

An intergovernmental meeting had been scheduled since the previous year. Our embassy was in full organisation mode, liaising with the Élysée Palace, and with Dublin, and arranging a luncheon for President Giscard d'Estaing. The evening before, our Taoiseach, Charles J. Haughey, had been entertained to dinner by the president, and now it was our turn. We had been left in no doubt by Haughey's office in Dublin that he expected the Connemara roast lamb to be accompanied by Château Lynch-Bages.

I had only met and spoken to Haughey that one time in Saint-Cloud racecourse, but I often thought of the consequences that had flowed from that day. As Bill O'Neill had once predicted, Haughey was now popular across a wide political spectrum. His personal wealth and ostentatious lifestyle, funded by sources that were never explained, and his reputation as a bully and a womaniser, endeared him to those sections of the electorate in need of a certain kind of reflected glory. His was the overwhelming presence in Irish politics and would remain so for another ten years, until the extent of his dishonesty would eventually undo him, and he would leave politics in terminal disgrace.

I was almost late. Georgie had awoken with a fever and, since Sugar didn't want to leave her and it was Nurse Fleming's day off, I hurried down to the local pharmacy in Saint-Cloud. By the time I'd waited, and was served, got home and set out for central Paris, an hour had gone by. I jumped from the Metro at Étoile and ran the last five hundred yards, just as the Taoiseach's cavalcade was pulling in. A sizeable crowd, including television crews, had assembled. Our ambassador, waiting by the entrance, frowned in my direction as I hurried inside. I went up the stairs, two at a time, and took my place in the long, gloriously appointed room whose generous windows overlooked the 16th arrondissement. The atmosphere was almost skittish: all the embassy staff, especially the women, wanted to shake hands with Charlie Haughey.

Would he remember our previous meeting, I wondered as the flashes from the cameras outside reflected upwards? I was sure he could not forget it, given all that had followed, but, equally, I decided, he would never take the risk of engaging with me. On the other hand, given his new position as Taoiseach, Haughey would now be the recipient of state secrets and sensitive information. Was there a file somewhere, marked 'Top Secret', which located me in south Armagh on St Stephen's Day 1976? As I was speculating how far up the political tree that file might have climbed, the doors opened and our ambassador appeared with Charles J. Haughey beside him.

He was smaller than I'd remembered, but just as fit, with bounce and vitality, a Napoleonic-type force that instantly flew around the room. Because I had been late, I was on the end of the receiving line, beside Philippe, our concierge. The Taoiseach was in jocular form, making a point of engaging with every member of staff to whom he was introduced, in the cases of the women taking their hand in both of his and, in one instance, kissing the fingertips of a very attractive young secretary. Five paces from where I stood, I became aware that he had seen me. My size has always made me hard to miss. His eyes locked into their hooded blinkers and his smile dried up. All at once, from outside, came a polite round of applause, which meant that the President of France had arrived. Haughey turned in my direction. His expression was that of a bird of prey that has scented danger. I nodded. His mouth took on a grim set. Then he turned on his heel and walked swiftly from the room.

7

EN ROUTE TO IRELAND

April 1982
Easter

Although we had spent weekends in the Loire and in Burgundy, it was Normandy we liked best. On the Wednesday of Easter week, we drove on the new AutoRoute to a hotel we knew in Thury-Harcourt, not far from Caen, which left us with a short run the next day to the ferry at Cherbourg. I had booked three rooms and the five of us went out to dinner, at which Emmet and I ate wild boar. Afterwards, we left the children and Nurse Fleming playing Scrabble, and walked through the town to a bridge where moonlight danced on a fast-running river.

'I've been thinking about Waterloo,' I said. 'When we get home, I'm going to sell it. I want to buy in Paris, but I don't want to borrow.'

Sugar thought for a moment. 'Sell all of it?'

'We might keep a few acres, in case the children want to come back and build there.'

'What about us?'

'We can stay with them.'

She lit a cigarette and tossed the match over the parapet. 'We've been away a long time. You should get advice.'

'From whom?'

'I don't know – Bobby Gillece? He's your family, after all.'

'I'm not sure I want to involve him.'

'Why not?'

'Oh, I don't know. It's complicated.'

She leant against the stonework and blew smoke towards the sky. 'May I ask you something? Something quite personal?'

'By all means.'

'Last time we were home, I came across some old photographs that I assume belonged to your parents. One of them was taken on the quay in Waterford when you were twelve or thirteen. You're standing beside a woman who I'm pretty sure is Bobby Gillece's wife, in other words, your father's sister Kate.'

I didn't know what was coming next. 'Yes?'

'She's most attractive. It took me a minute to work out who she was – I mean, when I last saw her she was enormously fat, but this woman in the picture is really striking.'

'I don't remember.'

'Your arm is around her waist. She's looking at the camera, but you're looking at her.'

'I was just about to get on a boat and go away to school.'

'I'm curious,' Sugar said. 'Were you in love with her?'

I laughed. 'She was my aunt!'

'So what?'

'I was a child! What's all this about?'

'I just wondered, that's all,' said Sugar sweetly and flicked her cigarette away.

Throughout the sea passage next day, I kept thinking of my last encounter with Bobby, in his pub, when his guard had dropped for an instant, and I thought I had seen what he really felt about me. But now Sugar had made me think again about the reasons behind his dislike. Perhaps it had nothing to do with Iggy. I already knew that Bobby had seen me kissing Kate on the quayside, all those years before, and, although he had been drunk when he told me, he had implied that his marriage with Kate had never been consummated. What had really happened, I wondered? Had Kate's ancient affection for me become an issue for them? She could have, for example, during a row, or at a time when Bobby might have denigrated me in her presence, eulogised me. And he might have flung this back at her when, perhaps, she might have withheld intimacy from him on the basis that he was drunk, which he frequently was. Auntie Kate may well have compared Bobby to me if their failure to have children was his. I was speculating, but I thought I could suddenly understand Bobby's hostility in a new light and, if this were true, then my deeper fears around him were unfounded.

As the children watched excitedly for a glimpse of Ireland next morning, and the first bumps of the Saltees appeared off the port bow, I asked myself how Alison would have dealt with the situation. She would have breezed ahead, just as I was doing, I decided, remaining positive, never offering the enemy a faltering stride. Which was also how the Captain would have done it, I reflected, and as I did so, I grasped in a moment of long overdue comprehension, why I had loved Alison so much.

8

WATERLOO FARM

Easter 1982

Everywhere I looked I saw my parents, and our horses, and Alison carrying out a tray of home-made lemonade to the tennis court, now a pasture for mountain ewes. We put our backs into wiping mould from leathers and fabrics, and setting fires and opening windows, and cleaning up the shit of the sparrows that had become trapped inside and died horribly around the windows. And yet, the old charm of the place began to creep over me, even as I picked up the telephone and rang Bobby Gillece.

An hour later I was sitting in his kitchen.

'Great to see you,' he said. 'Long time – too long.' My sniper's sight could see no chink in his smile, which, when added to my seaborne epiphany, made me wonder how wrongly I had judged him. 'How's it going in Gay Paree?'

I drank tea as I told him of our new life, and how it seemed to suit us. I told him of our decision.

'Well, well, well,' he said, 'I never thought you'd let it go.'

'It's just a bloody house.'

'All the same – but fair play to you.'

'We'll keep a few acres for the kids.'

'Great idea. Keep the name going up there.'

I tried to see beyond Bobby's natural deviousness, to see what this news really meant to him, but I could make out nothing other than surprise, polite regret and a swift series of calculations to see how he could benefit financially.

'Waterford has never been the same for me, to be honest, since Iggy left,' I said, watching closely to see how he would react to such a shameless assertion.

He coughed. 'I know what you mean.'

'All I'm saying is that, looking back, when we were all here together was the happiest time of my life.'

Bobby coughed again, but I could see nothing in his face but faint puzzlement.

'So,' he said, rubbing his hands, 'how long are you home for?'

'Ten days.'

'Then we'd better get things in motion. I've the right man for you. He has contacts longer than your arm, and you can trust him, which is the main thing. I'll set something up for next week.'

We all went to mass in Ballyhale on Easter morning, where the smells and sideways glances, the familiar profiles, even the sound of feet shuffling towards the altar rail for Communion were exactly as I remembered them. Georgie had become a Holy Communicant; she wore a simple white veil as she stood in line to receive the host with myself and Nurse Fleming. Sugar, as a Protestant, could not receive Communion, and remained in the pew with Emmet. He had become quite independent in his attitudes, including his view of religion, which was, from what I could gather, one of indifference.

We drove home on the narrow road that sliced across open country towards our mountain. Sun and colour exploded to reveal ewes and their lambs by twinkling gullies. I would always love this place for its beauty, serenity and gut-tightening isolation, but now I would have to love it from afar. Those who lived in a place permanently seldom appreciated it, I reasoned; my childhood here was stored away in careful images, caverns full of them, enough to get me through to old age. Much as the sight of our lake, as it now appeared, and the wash of valley below it begged me to hold them tight for ever, I knew in my blood that my time there was up.

It was warm enough at lunchtime on Easter Monday to light a fire by the lake and grill the trout Emmet had caught the night before. I sensed the heady feeling of a group about to embark on a new adventure. Although the children were polite enough to behave as if they enjoyed being in their ancestral home – a Captain-like term if ever there was one – more than once I heard them chatting quietly about Paris. That was exciting, for it seemed to prove where our real home was and that my decision to sell Waterloo was the right one.

We discussed the piece of land I had earmarked to keep, on the west side of the lake with views on a good day to the river, but I knew now that these European children found my plans for a lifeline to this lovely barren spot at best endearing. Sugar and I drank a bottle of Montrachet.

'Do you want to come to this meeting tomorrow?'

She looked at me. 'And spend an hour with Mr Gillece? No thank you very much.'

'It's your property, too.'

'Not really, Marty,' she said. 'Anyway, you don't need me there.'

A dramatic sunset set the hills on fire. I sat with a drink outside the hall door, a fleece around my shoulders, imagining from time to time that Oscar, my childhood dog, was near at hand.

9

WATERFORD

Easter Tuesday 1982

I had driven out across the soldier course of cobbles that marked the boundary between the gravel sweep around the house and the rough, crushed flint of our so-called avenue, and was almost at the bridge beneath which the water from the lake regained its status as a stream and flowed on downhill through tens of thousands of acres of heather and rock before eventually uniting with countless others of its kind before becoming a tributary of the River Suir, when they stopped me. I might not have seen them had I been looking the other way, or if the morning sun had blinded my wing-mirror with its radiance. In the moment that I did see them, running and waving for me to stop, perhaps within that moment it might have been possible to ignore what I saw – for I knew from the way they were attired what they wanted – and I could have driven on alone, continued as I had intended, by myself, to finish what I alone had started.

'We're coming too,' Sugar said.

They had decided at the last moment, or Sugar had,

that Georgie should look for material for the skirt she needed in the drapery shop on Broad Street. It is only in retrospect that one analyses these tiny moments, like atoms, which contain within themselves the entire universe, or its destruction. We drove uphill and across the long ridge where I used to shoot rabbits. Mist clung to this part of mountain flank, which my mother had so admired for its gentians. I lit a cigarette as we climbed again, the mist cleared, and at the Door, where two rocks formed a portal, the town came into view and we began our descent.

The auctioneer, Mr Gargan, had an office in Michael Street, up from the Apple Market. He was, of course, a crony of Bobby's, who had once been in that business himself. Allowing Bobby to be involved in the sale, something he had readily agreed to, was a straightforward wager: his visceral feelings about me, from wherever they sprang, would be put on hold for as long as there was cash to be made.

'Oh, there's Mr Gillece,' Georgie said as we came in past the railway station.

'Where?' I said, looking everywhere.

'He just passed us. He was going out the Dublin road.'

'He couldn't have been.'

'I think he was. His wife was with him.'

The child had to be wrong. A hundred men in Waterford looked like Bobby Gillece, although not many women looked like my Aunt Kate.

'I don't even know if this drapery shop still exists,' Sugar said.

'I'm sure it does,' I said.

'Is it still called the Misses Flynn?' she asked.

'I wonder who the Misses Flynn were,' Georgie said.

'I wonder,' I said as we crossed the bridge and I pulled up on the Quay. 'Look, I'm going to walk from here. You take the car.'

'Where will we meet you?' Sugar asked as she climbed from the passenger seat to the driver's in an agile movement that made me smile.

'There's parking in the Apple Market, near where I'm meeting this Gargan man,' I said and blew them kisses. 'Meet you there in an hour.'

I walked into O'Connell Street. Bobby's Bar was twenty yards from the corner. It was quarter past eleven. I smelt stale beer and cigarette smoke. Two men sat in a little patch of sunlight with large bottles of stout before them.

'Hello.'

A youth I did not recognise, no more than sixteen, stood up from behind the bar.

'Is Bobby around?'

'Bobby's not here.'

'Is Mrs Gillece here?'

'No, they've both gone off for a few days.'

I stared at him. 'Gone off?'

'Yeah.'

'Where?'

'I don't know. He just told me they were going off for a few days.'

'By the sound of him, I'd say they're heading for Liverpool,' said one of the men from his place by the window. 'Aintree races. Bobby backed Red Rum a few years ago, you know.'

All at once, I could not calculate fast enough. 'Where's the phone?'

'There's a coin box in the hall,' the youth said.

'I haven't time for the coin box,' I said, raising the counter flap. 'I'm his cousin, Marty. Where's the bloody phone?'

'In Bobby's office,' he said and pointed to the nook in the hall behind the bar.

'You must have a few tips,' one of the men called out.

Bobby's so-called office consisted of a desk with untidy mounds of what looked like suppliers' invoices, bank statements, beer mats, pens, rubber bands, a diary and a telephone. I had written the number of the auctioneers on a tear of paper.

'Gargan Auctioneers.'

'Mr John Gargan, my name is Ransom, I have an appointment this morning.'

'Ah, Mr Ransom, I'm glad you rang. Mr Gargan unfortunately has had to cancel. He's unwell. He apologises.'

Everywhere I looked, everything I saw, sucked out my oxygen. 'Is Mr Bobby Gillece there?'

'Who?'

Doing deals like this had kept Bobby afloat all his life. He was in Gargan's office. With Kate, my aunt. Before heading off to the Aintree races.

'Bobby Gillece.'

'I'm sorry, Mr Ransom, there's no one here. Maybe if you call back ... Hello?'

I could not hear her. My attention was locked on a faded photograph, pinned to the back of the door, of three teenage boys, guns in their belts, standing beside the running boards of a Morris Oxford Saloon. Scrawled along the bottom of the picture was 'The Flying Squad'. Ted and Bobby. My hand was shaking as I removed the photograph and held it under the light. The third young man was smiling at the camera in a way that made it look as if he knew what the photographer was thinking. Even though the picture was blurred on that side, and he was no more than sixteen years old, it could only have been Bill O'Neill.

I burst from the fetid pub and ran the length of O'Connell Street. How could I ever have doubted the truth? On the gentle curve of George's Street, I almost fell. They would have driven directly to the Apple Market, walked up to Broad Street and would now be inside the drapery with its subdued light where I had often idled while my mother had fingered bolts of cloth. I could imagine exactly Sugar's surprised expression as I entered. How long did it take women to select fabric? Bells chimed as I pushed the door in.

'Sugar!'

I was struggling for breath as I took in the layout of the shop, its broad wooden counters and long shelves, the somehow comforting ambience and redolence of cloth, the floor linoleum that was reflecting the yellow sunlight that seeped in through protective plastic stuck to the street door's glass panels.

'May I help you?'

'I'm looking for my wife, my daughter.'

'You're Mr Ransom, aren't you?'

I had no idea who she was, or how she knew me. She was small, and smiling, wearing a white blouse, in her late twenties.

'Yes – have they just left?'

'Who?'

'My wife, my daughter. They were here to look for cloth. For a skirt. When did they leave?'

'They haven't been here, Mr Ransom, but if you'd like to wait for them, please take a seat.'

'They haven't been here?'

'No. Not yet. Can I say something?'

'What?'

She took a deep breath. 'You probably don't remember me, but I'm Peggy Flynn. My father, John Flynn, used to ride horses. Do you remember the day of the point-to-point in Waterloo? In the snow?'

It took all my resources to stand there. 'Yes.'

She was weeping now. 'You were so kind to me that day, Mr Ransom, I'll never forget it and I'm so ashamed that I never thanked you. I was only ten, but that's no excuse.'

I gaped at her. 'Your father ...'

She nodded and fought back her tears.

Dada! No, please, Dada! No!

'Miss Flynn, forgive me, but you'll have to excuse me, I must find my wife,' I said and lurched back out to the street.

I ran straight up Broad Street. Dead ahead, through gaps in the skyline, the rooftops of Ballybricken appeared, rearing over the town. I knew now, and I prayed: not to God, for he would surely never have me, but to the Captain, who would understand, and to Alison, all-knowing and now all-seeing Alison, whom I still loved, whom I now begged for the sake of that love to prove me wrong. I prayed, too, to Iggy, even at this late hour, even given how it had ended between us, for I could still remind him that I had done the right thing that day at the pub on the border, something he should weigh in my favour. I had given him a chance and now I wanted one from him.

With each stride as I ran into Michael Street, busy with shoppers, I was calling out. Sugar! Sugar! People stared at me, but not for long, for when the whooshing wind came and the shop windows on either side all disintegrated, everyone was thrown flat, faces down, hands on their heads, melons and turnips spinning, broken eggs with vivid yolks that I sprang over. Or thought I did, but could not have, for I was pinned to the street, as if a foot were on my neck, cold stone to my lips, as the ground yawed like a thimble in mercury. Much as I tried to get up, the weight of the explosion refused to yield, until eventually my deafness eased and I could taste my blood. My knees were bared where the fabric of my trousers had been ripped, so that when I eventually knelt sharp pain scalded my legs. My shoes were gone. In stockinged feet, I swayed upright, and stumbled on through the dazed and tingling aftermath. Dust hung in a cloud over that part of Waterford, where the wail of house alarms had broken out like geese in fright, as stunned men and women, some with blackened faces, struggled where they lay. I was shouting and calling out as I began to run. I didn't want to ever get there and find what I knew awaited me. I wanted to run for ever, never arriving, always suspended, praying for the mercy that would never be given, caught in the perpetual momentum that would spare me. I ran and ran.

Epilogue

Guelph Line, Campbellville, Ontario

The Recent Past

As she busies herself in the kitchen, awaiting the intercom that will announce the arrival of the doctor at the road gate, her ancient life – for that is what it seems like now – hurries through Nurse Dora Fleming's mind.

In her head, doctors are still venerable gynaecologists, men with rooms in Fitzwilliam Square, who do their ward rounds in beautifully tailored English worsteds and crisp linen. She could have walked straight into a job in the bank – first in her class with the Presentation nuns, such immaculate handwriting – but she chose midwifery. Her mother was glacial in her disapproval. She had wanted her to remain in Tralee and marry a well-to-do farmer, probably a client of the bank whose job offer awaited her acceptance. Mrs Fleming had imagined Dora the mistress of her own fields, surrounded by sleek cattle, and keenly wished for the affirmation of her daughter's place in society that such circumstances would bestow.

In the autumn of 1961 she was sent from Dublin to the delivery ward of the hospital in Waterford, as the

271

relief for a nurse who had herself given birth, and after Christmas out to Waterloo, as a temporary help for Mrs Ransom and her baby boy. Such jobs were looked upon as something of a holiday; only the gentry could afford the services of a personal nurse, and although the Ransoms had no money, they were thought of as gentry. Thus, she arrived into the kind of setting that her mother's ambitions had always imagined. She never left.

She adored Sugar. Her poise, her beauty. She took shy notice of how she dressed and copied her style in small, discreet ways. Never in her life had she come across such grace as when Sugar played tennis. Sitting in Fitzwilliam, with the children, watching their mother qualify for a tournament, she felt a sense of possession that had never left her.

He has recently begun to talk about death. Not in the sense that he fears it, but with the realisation that only with death can he escape from this continuum. He still retains the belief of his childhood faith that there is another world where those he loves await him. He has made a list of their names.

'A bloody long list, isn't it, Nurse Fleming?'

All outside is quiet. He has remained upstairs, since they have agreed that the doctor will want to examine him in detail. She hears a shout of frustration from the bathroom overhead as he knocks some part of himself, but never once in all the time since they moved here has he asked her for assistance. And never has he addressed her other than as 'Nurse Fleming'.

All those years ago, when speed was of the essence and a lot of big decisions had to be made quickly, it was because of Emmet that she stayed on, at first. Her instinct told her it was the right thing to do. Events moved so fast. After the funerals, conducted in private, they had returned briefly to Waterloo, but the Gardaí had not been able to guarantee his safety. One night, without warning – at least she had not been warned – they left the south-east in a convoy, and drove to an RAF base outside Belfast. In the months that followed, as they were moved from place to place in England, a diversionary measure, it was to her that Emmet clung. He saw his father as a stranger. He was twenty years old and wanted to return to Paris, to his girlfriend, which he eventually did, a month before they left for Canada. It was Emmet who persuaded her to go with his father, in the end. He did not want her to come to Paris, and Dora Fleming realised that she had nowhere else to go.

His bathwater trundles out beneath the floor of the kitchen. She raises her head. Up on Guelph Line, a truck has backfired. She is wearing a white day-coat of nylon fabric, the way a nurse should appear in a professional situation. In the kitchen, on a tray, she has laid out teacups and plates and a dish with cookies. The teapot awaits charging from the electric kettle that is already whistling. She will add a jug of cream, from the fridge, just to show the doctor a little bit of Ireland, when his examination is completed. She is looking forward to her chat with him, and hearing about his other reassessments, and being proud of how the boss compares to other people. Later, when the doctor has left, they will have a drink on the deck, just the two of them, and discuss what the doctor has said. A gin for him; for her, a single glass of white wine. Anyone might imagine them to be a married couple.

The sudden sound of a car can be heard on the gravel. She has taken a step towards the door, when she pauses. Did the intercom sound? She is so used to the sequence, that now she cannot remember. Maybe it did sound, but the din from the kettle meant that she could not hear it. The procedure in such a case has been made very clear: if in doubt, you pick up the intercom phone and talk to the security detail up on the road.

And now the doorbell rings. The three sets of locks have to be dealt with. Nurse Fleming should lift the phone and check, but then – is it polite to keep a doctor waiting?

Thanks To

Carol Cunningham for her love and wisdom; Frances O'Rourke, Michael Kennedy, Naomi Powell, Maria White and Jonathan Williams; my editor Moira Forsyth, Bob Davidson and everyone at Sandstone Press; my agent, Caroline Montgomery of Rupert Crew Ltd., Shaun Boylan, Ciaran Byrne, Tom Cunningham, Eamon Delaney, Ruth Dudley Edwards, Ashley Hall, Anthony Haughey, Eddie McGrath, Kevin Myers, Olive Nagle, John Owen-Jones, Julian Walton, Dick Warner and the very many other people who so generously helped me.